Glendale County is Paige Wojtyla's first published book. She attended the University of Winnipeg in the 1980s and Memorial University of Newfoundland in the 1990s. She started writing *Glendale County* when her husband became ill and finished it shortly after he died. *Glendale County* is dedicated to Paige's husband who encouraged her to fulfill her dream as a writer. She currently lives in Moncton, New Brunswick, Canada with her two precious cats, Julie and Kingsley.

This book is dedicated to my late husband, Roderick Patrick Roulette.

Paige Wojtyla

GLENDALE COUNTY

AUSTIN MACAULEY PUBLISHERS™
LONDON * CAMBRIDGE * NEW YORK * SHARJAH

This is a work of fiction. Names, characters, businesses, places, events, locales, and incidents are either the products of the author's imagination or used in a fictitious manner. Any resemblance to actual persons, living or dead, or actual events is purely coincidental.

Ordering Information
Quantity sales: Special discounts are available on quantity purchases by corporations, associations, and others. For details, contact the publisher at the address below.

Publisher's Cataloging-in-Publication data
Wojtyla, Paige
Glendale County

ISBN 9781643788999 (Paperback)
ISBN 9781645365549 (ePub e-book)

Library of Congress Control Number: 2023919667

www.austinmacauley.com/us

First Published 2024
Austin Macauley Publishers LLC
40 Wall Street 33rd Floor, Suite 3302
New York, NY 10005
USA

mail-usa@austinmacauley.com
+1 (646) 5125767

I would like to thank Austin Macauley Publishers for assisting me with the publication of *Glendale County*, and am grateful to my husband who encouraged me to fulfill my dream as a writer.

Chapter 1

Mary Anne was a million miles away, lost in a daydream. "You're starting up again!" Mary Anne's mother yelled from her rocking chair in the living room.

"Starting up what?" Mary Anne yelled back, standing at the kitchen sink of the small yellow trailer, finishing the supper dishes.

"Starting up that staring out the window thing you do," Marjorie said, re-rolling one of her curlers. Mary Anne's stepfather, Erno Federno, stubbed out a cigarette in the ashtray. Empty beer cans lay scattered on the floor.

"Mary Anne, could you run to the store and get more beer?" Erno asked, and belched.

"I'll tell you what," Mary Anne said, turning to her mother. "I'll go get Erno's beer, and then take you to the casino. That will give you time to take those God-awful rollers out of your hair. They're a fire hazard," Mary Anne said, aiming a can of hairspray at her mother like it was a fire extinguisher. They both laughed.

"Just what I need, my gambling fix," Marjorie replied, getting up slowly, favoring her right hip. She went over to the tiny kitchen and took out a jar of instant coffee and a mug. Then she plugged in the kettle and while it was heating up, took out her large curlers. Meanwhile, Mary Anne was already down the front steps and out to her black Chevy which seemed to have a mind of its own. Sometimes it started and sometimes it didn't. This time, she got lucky and the motor turned over and purred like a kitten, a kitten with a raspy throat, no less.

Soon Mary Anne was on her way, singing along with Eddie Rabbitt, It's a Rainy Night, which was playing on the radio. At a red light, a red mustang convertible with the top down pulled up alongside her. It was packed like sardines with a rowdy bunch of teenagers. A spiky-haired rock star wannabe in the backseat suddenly stood up and mooned her. They all laughed. Then the light turned green and the convertible sped away. A man in the car behind Mary Anne honked impatiently. "Lady, I don't have all day!" he shouted.

Mary Anne gave him the finger and took her time applying some ruby red lipstick. Then she blew him a kiss and turned left at the next block into the liquor store parking lot. To her surprise, he pulled into the parking lot too.

"Hi, I'm Professor West," he said as he got out of his car.

"As in *Wild, Wild West?*" Mary Anne asked, not breaking stride as she waltzed into the liquor store and headed for the beer section.

"Something like that," Professor West laughed, smiling warmly. He looked about forty, but maybe he was prematurely balding. Mary Anne was thirty-two.

"I teach creative writing once a week," the Professor said, handing her a couple of his business cards. She took them and put them in her purse where they were swallowed up among half a dozen tubes of lipstick, mascara and pancake makeup. She opened her mouth to speak but couldn't find her voice and promptly closed it again.

The Professor was way out of her league, the type of guy who dressed down and was a bit too polite. By the time Mary Anne paid for Erno's beer, the elusive Professor West had already driven away into the sunset.

Chapter 2

It was Glendale, Saskatchewan, Canada. The year was 1987. Mary Anne pulled into the driveway and sat in her truck for a while, mesmerized by the twinkling Christmas lights that illuminated the tiny porch. She had lived in that trailer for the past fifteen years. Mary Anne got out and reached into the back of the cab for the two twelve packs. She brought them inside and put them in the fridge, but not before tossing a beer to Erno, who caught it at the last moment.

"Hey, watch it!" he hollered, but his attention was soon on the TV, flicking through the stations searching for the sports channel. Marjorie was waiting patiently by the door ready to go. She smelled like rose petals and Salon Selectives hairspray. Her lucky shawl with the hand-sewn silver and gold sequins to pick up the casino lights was wrapped around her tiny shoulders. *That had better be the only thing she picks up*, Mary Anne thought.

As if reading her thoughts, Marjorie said defensively, "I'll have you know that Maybelline Levine next door asked me to make her a shawl just like it." Maybelline, affectionately known as the Cat Lady, was a widow who used to collect men, but now collected strays of the feline persuasion.

"Hi, I'm Maybelline," she'd say when you met her. "Don't judge."

"Feeling lucky?" Mary Anne asked as they pulled into the Lucky Slots Casino. She stopped at the taxi stand and got out the step stool. Then she went around to the passenger side and helped Marjorie down.

"Why don't you get a smaller vehicle? I'm not getting any taller, you know."

"I will if you hit the jackpot." It was a Saturday night. They walked into the crowded casino arm in arm. There were blackjack tables and slot machines, and off to the right was the Lucky Stars Lounge that lived up to its name.

"This machine looks promising," Marjorie said, batting her eyelashes. Her eyes lit up as she slid into the seat and fed the machine a couple of $10 bills.

"I'll be in the lounge," Mary Anne said reassuringly, kissing her mother on the cheek. "Don't spend too much money. We still need a place to stay."

"What will you have?" asked a young man behind the bar. He was wearing black pants and a black vest, and sporting a white, long-sleeved shirt. His black bowtie, slightly askew, matched his equally lopsided grin.

"Anything fizzy," Mary Anne said, touching up her lip gloss. "No, on second thought, I think I'll have a double espresso." Mr. Bowtie left and a short time later returned with a tiny cup. "See that lady over there with the curls? That's Marjorie, my mother," Mary Anne said, pointing. "She's going to hit the jackpot and win me a whole new life."

"Oh yeah?"

"And why not? By the way, what's your name?"

"Thomas."

"As in *Doubting Thomas*?"

"Something like that," Thomas replied, softening. He moved to the other end of the counter to serve an old couple who had just sat down. They were holding hands. *Look at those two*, Mary Anne thought, staring into space. *Still in love.*

Chapter 3

"In what universe?" Marjorie asked, poking her daughter in the ribs.

"Knock it off, Mother. Did you win anything?"

"Nah, an old man with bad gas and even worse breath sat down at the machine next to me. I couldn't concentrate."

"So that explains it. Erno, I blew all our money because of gas. You'd better come up with a better alibi than that."

"I only spent twenty dollars," Marjorie said defensively, and winked at Mary Anne. It was a secret wink they shared, meaning that she had stuffed the other couple of twenties in her bra so Erno wouldn't find them. It was the last place he'd look because sex between them had gone out the window years ago.

Mary Anne helped Marjorie into the truck and soon they were headed back home. *Forever Young* by Rod Stewart was playing on the radio. "Say, I met someone at the liquor store earlier today," Mary Anne said above the music.

"Was he cute?"

"Nothing to write home about," Mary Anne said casually, looking at herself in the rear-view mirror and brushing away an imaginary eyelash.

"Why don't you settle down like all your friends?"

"And where are they now, Mom? Divorced? Look at Julie Sykes. Family Services took away her babies. And what about Heather Morechild? Her old man rolled the car and her whole family was wiped out in a cruel twist of fate. Poor Heather had to be dragged off to the insane asylum. It was God-awful. Why go there at all, Mother, or do you want me to end up just like you?"

As soon as the words were out of her mouth, she regretted it. Marjorie pursed her lips tightly and for a moment looked like she was going to slap her daughter across the face. It was the same old argument. "I'm sorry, Mother." Mary Anne was the one constant in Marjorie's broken life and she knew it. She reached over and gave Marjorie's arthritic hand a squeeze. "I met a man today, Mother. His name is Professor West, and he teaches creative writing at the college." Mary Anne rummaged in her purse for his business card, but couldn't find it.

"Oh, that's okay," Marjorie said, with a hint of resignation in her voice. "A literary man, I like that. Professor West can help me write my Will," she added matter-of-factly as they pulled into the driveway. "Now help me down from this Godforsaken beast!" Mary Anne helped her mother inside, mother and daughter changing roles, mother and daughter afraid of change.

Chapter 4

"Mercy!" Erno moaned the next morning. He was wedged between the couch and coffee table. He must have rolled off reaching for the ashtray and passed out.

"One day you are going to burn this place down," Marjorie scolded. "I'm too old to babysit."

"I hope you have insurance, Mother."

"It's not the trailer I'm worried about. It's the family albums and your grandmother's bone china dishes. They're priceless."

"Why don't we get a dog? It can bark if the trailer catches on fire. We can even teach it how to call 911 like I saw on TV."

Marjorie abruptly changed the subject, as was her habit. "Why don't you give that creative writing professor a call? You've got so much talent. You just need to harness it."

"Very funny," Mary Anne said and kissed her mother on the cheek. Erno had somehow managed to drag himself over to the kitchen table where he sat nursing a hangover beer. He peered over the top of his black-rimmed glasses and looked up briefly from *The Glendale Herald*. He read the obituaries, the sport's section, the funnies, and the classifieds, before surrendering the newspaper to Marjorie.

Just then, there was a knock on the screen door. It was Al Critch. Al was a handyman who knew a lot about a lot of things. He came in handy.

"You don't have to knock," Erno said without looking up from his newspaper.

Al stepped inside and wiped his boots on the welcome mat. "Don't bother taking your boots off," Marjorie said dismissively. "The floors are filthy anyway."

"Al, are you still seeing Maybelline?" Erno asked. Al and Maybelline had been dating on and off for several years.

Al leaned against the kitchen counter facing the couple. "Yeah, same old, same old. Poor old gal had to put Tom Jones down. A fur ball got stuck in his throat, or something to that effect. All she's got left are two old Toms, Earle and Tyler, 'cuz Wailin' Jennings got runned over." Maybelline's cats were all tomcats and named after musicians. Earle and Tyler were named after *Steve Earle* and Aerosmith's *Steven Tyler*. Some came to her as strays and others were dropped off at her doorstep. Earle and Tyler were litter mates and dropped off as kittens. Their eyes had barely opened when they arrived and Maybelline had to feed them with an eyedropper. Now geriatric and arthritic, they were still her babies. Time showed no mercy.

"When are you two getting hitched?" Erno asked Al who was pouring himself a cup of coffee.

"When the last of those blasted tomcats has gone to tomcat heaven. They're always in the bed. Can't sleep over for fear of squishing them. Darned woman'd never forgive me."

"You've got a point," Erno said, looking into his empty coffee mug, lost in thought. He looked like a psychic reading coffee grounds. "Life's a bitch, ain't it?" Without giving Al time to respond, Erno continued, "Say, want a beer? Saved you one."

"Nah, I'm on my way over to the Periwinkles to mow the quack grass. Mind if I borrow the newspaper?"

"Sure, go ahead," Erno said, gesturing toward the Glendale Herald on the table. "Nothing much ever happens here anyway. Just put it in the mailbox afterward. Marjorie hasn't read it yet."

Al wore coveralls every day and carried around a hammer in a side pocket. A pencil was stuck behind his ear just to remind dim-witted folks that he was the handyman and was on call 24/7, 365 days of the year. In case folks in Glendale needed something hammered, he was the handyman to call and pencil in on the calendar. He could even provide the pencil. He was that handy. And to all the Maybellines around town, Al could even fix that. With a wink, Al Critch, the handyman, was gone.

Chapter 5

"I wish I had his energy," Erno said, getting up to use the washroom. He closed the door and soon Marjorie could hear the shower running. She looked in the dresser drawers for a fresh undershirt and boxers, as well as a clean t-shirt and pair of pants. Then she fished out a matching pair of support stockings. When she was done, Marjorie opened the washroom door and ceremoniously set the clothes on the dryer like he was a Ken Barbie doll from the projects, a bit worse for wear, threadbare, but clean.

"Put these on!" she hollered, though she doubted he could hear her over the sound of the shower. "You have a doctor's appointment today," she reminded him and shut the door behind her.

Mary Anne had an early shift at Dino's Diner. Portions were double-sized and nobody left hungry. Today they were short-staffed and she was run off her feet. "Will that be everything?" Mary Anne asked when Nancy Gilmoss came to the cash register to pay for her breakfast. Nancy was a schoolteacher at Glendale Elementary and had been there for twenty-two years.

"Yes, thank you," Nancy replied, forever gracious.

"Say, Nancy," Mary Anne continued, "have you ever heard of somebody by the last name of West?"

"West? That name does sound familiar. I'll look over some old class yearbooks if you like. How old did you say he is?"

"I didn't, but I'd say he's fortyish, give or take."

"Alright then," Nancy said in a hushed voice, "I'll see what I can dig up."

Chapter 6

The end of Mary Anne's shift finally arrived when Wendy Stump, her replacement, put on her apron. Wendy was jealous of Mary Anne because Mary Anne got better tips. Mary Anne had worked for the previous owner who sold Dino's diner in a vicious divorce, but thankfully, the new owner, God bless his soul, had kept the same restaurant name, menu, and staff.

His real name was Karlos Miskatorus, but everybody called him Dino, and the name stuck. Dino worked the kitchen grill. Nobody got fired, but Dino was tough to work for. He'd bark out orders from behind the counter to embarrass his staff in front of customers. Whenever the dishwasher broke down, the dishes had to be washed by hand. That was when Al Critch was called in. "Just leave your hammer under the cash register," Dino would say. "It makes a bad impression."

Mary Anne waltzed out the door swinging her handbag. The day was sunny and she was glad to be getting off work. She always parked right in front of the diner on Main Street, as if the spot was reserved exclusively for her. Looking out the window of her Chevy, she could see Dino and Wendy squaring off, no doubt over Wendy's chronic lateness. Babysitter troubles. In a way, Mary Anne felt sorry for her. She went back into the diner. "Wendy," she began, "do you need a babysitter for your little girl—what's her name?"

"Belinda Jane," Wendy replied proudly, though still visibly frazzled, "and yes I do need a babysitter. My last sitter quit when she got a job at the potato chip factory. Before that, I left Belinda Jane at Shady Acres Nursing Home with Gran but the nurses complained. 'We're not babysitters,' the Head nurse with big boobs would say unsympathetically, 'Leave that brat here again and you'll be hearing from Social Services!'."

"I'll see what I can do," Mary Anne promised. "You can't keep showing up here late every day."

"I know, I know," Wendy said apologetically, pouring coffee for a couple of construction workers sitting at the counter. They were eating corned beef on rye with deli-style coleslaw and pan fries.

"Take care," Mary Anne said, and left again. Then it hit her. Maybelline, the Cat Lady, why of course. She provided the homemade pies for Dino's diner. Maybe she would have time to babysit a few nights a week?

Chapter 7

Ten minutes later, Mary Anne was pulling into her own driveway. She parked and hopped out, then walked over to Maybelline's trailer next door. The chimes overhead jingled in the breeze. She rang the doorbell. Once. Twice. The smell of cat pee and freshly baked apple pie made her feel slightly nauseated. After what seemed like an eternity, the door opened.

"Am I ever glad to see you!" Maybelline exclaimed, starved for company. "What brings you by? More pie?" The Cat Lady laughed at her own rhyme. "Come in. Come in."

Mary Anne stepped inside the door. "I can't stay. Wendy at the diner could use some help. She can't find a babysitter for Belinda Jane and Dino's running out of patience."

"How much can she pay?"

"You'll have to work that out between you two. Wendy's at the Diner now. Why don't you give her a call?"

Maybelline picked up the phone and dialed Dino's Diner as Mary Anne let herself out. *That's my good deed for the day*, Mary Anne thought. "No good deed goes unpunished," the devil whispered in her ear as she broke a heel and stumbled down the steps.

Back at the trailer, Mary Anne emptied her handbag on the bed, determined to find one of Professor West's business cards. She finally found one, tangled up in her hairbrush. It was smeared with lipstick. *Creative Writing Workshop taught by Professor West. Saturday night. Glendale Community College. 7 pm. Enquiries welcome.* Mary Anne dialed the number on the Professor's card.

The Professor answered on the first ring. "Hi, Mary Anne. You must be calling about the creative writing class. It starts tomorrow."

"How does this work? I've never taken a creative writing class before," Mary Anne admitted apologetically.

"Just bring some writing materials, and yourself, of course."

"Alright."

"Be there or be square," Professor West said before hanging up. Mary Anne put the receiver gently in its cradle. There was a hint of a smile on her face as she drifted off to sleep.

Chapter 8

Professor West entered the classroom in the basement of Glendale Community college. He wore denims, a white t-shirt, and a brown corduroy jacket with elbow patches. He set his leather briefcase on the desk and addressed the faces looking up at him. "Let's introduce ourselves. Hi. I'm Professor West, your creative writing professor." He passed out name tags and forms with a few background questions on them. After five minutes, the forms were filled out and handed back. Then Professor West pointed to the first student. We'll begin introductions, moving in a clockwise direction, starting with Sandy Brosben:

(1) Sandy Brosben: Glendale—housewife—bored
(2) Jane Stanley: Glendale—Retired office clerk—bored
(3) Peter Carmichael: Glendale—in therapy—looking to meet people
(4) Bella Porter: Glendale—widow—thought it might be interesting
(5) Mary Anne Tiski: Glendale—waitress—didn't really think it through too well
(6) Alex Remington: Glendale—unemployed—self-proclaimed genius— born to write

After introductions, Professor West circulated their first assignment: "For the next class," he instructed, "you are to write a short essay. Stick to what you know. Too many words, too few words, you are kicked out of the class." Jane and Sandy both giggled like a couple of schoolgirls. The Professor looked up at them with mock disapproval.

"I'm looking forward to our next class," Professor Pied Piper said enthusiastically. He picked up his briefcase and marched out of the classroom, with his young, and not so young protégés, trailing after him.

Chapter 9

Maybelline and Belinda Jane hit it off instantly. Wendy drove her daughter over to Maybelline's before her shifts at the diner and picked her up afterward. On one particular day when Wendy went to pick up Belinda Jane, she found her daughter fast asleep on the couch. One of Maybelline's tomcats was lying on her stomach. "Mommy, can I have this one? His name is Tyler. Please?" Belinda Jane begged, but all her mother would say was, "We'll see," which meant, "not likely."

On another occasion, Maybelline and Belinda Jane came to the door wearing mud masks. Their hair was wrapped in steamed towels. "Spa night!" Maybelline explained.

"And we made oatmeal raisin cookies too!" Belinda Jane pitched in excitedly. "Maybelline even let me eat cookie dough if I was good!"

Maybelline looked embarrassed. "Go wash your face. Don't keep your mother waiting."

Wendy laughed. "Don't worry. Your secret's safe with me." Afterward, she gathered up her daughter's belongings and passed Maybelline a crisp $20. "It's not much, but it should keep you in cat food and kitty litter until your next welfare cheque."

"You're lucky this mud mask has dried or I'd fling it at you!" Maybelline said, feigning hurt feelings. But the truth of the matter was that the Cat Lady made more money with her pie business than Wendy did as a waitress.

"See you tomorrow, Mebby." That was what Belinda Jane called Maybelline because she couldn't pronounce it. She hugged her sitter affectionately, and then followed her mother down the trailer steps.

The Cat Lady looked out the window as they drove away. *How life has a way of turning out*, she thought as she set down a fresh bowl of cream for Earle and Tyler. They always drank from the same bowl ever since she'd taken in the litter mates. Everything they did, they did together. And now they were lapping cream, side by side, furry shoulder to furry shoulder, purring appreciatively.

Chapter 10

Like clockwork, Al showed up at the trailer bright and early and helped himself to Erno's coffee. Whenever Erno made it, there were always a few grounds at the bottom of his coffee mug. "You have to rinse the basket," Marjorie would scold. "And don't overfill it."

"Mary Anne, how's that creative writing course going?" Al asked, changing the subject. "The whole town's talking about it."

"Great," Mary Anne said, not wishing to elaborate.

"Who all's in the class?" Marjorie asked, putting down four slices of bread in the double toaster and taking out a jar of raspberry jam. Mary Anne rattled off her classmates' names.

"I know Bella Porter. Why's that skank taking the course?"

"She thought it would be interesting."

"She would say that, that cougar. She went after Erno one time when I was at Bingo and you were working late."

"Mother, you never told me that."

"You never asked. Remember the time Bella had her house spray painted?"

"M-O-T-H-E-R, you didn't—?"

"—Karma," Marjorie cut in. "Had it coming to her."

Al popping a slice of toast into his mouth. "You say Alex Remington is in the class. Didn't he run for mayor?"

"He sure did," Erno joined in. "He did most of the campaigning himself. Waste of time if you ask me. Nobody wants a mayor who blows their own horn." There was a moment of silence, bordering on the reverent.

"Gotta run," Al said abruptly, looking at his watch. He drained his coffee mug and pulled something out of his teeth, likely coffee grounds. "Maybe I should sign up for that creative writing course too."

"Yeah, it's about time you gave that pencil behind your ear a workout. Never seen you use it yet," Marjorie teased. Al shook his head like he'd heard it all before, and helped himself to the newspaper on his way out the door.

Chapter 11

The creative writing course reconvened on Saturday night. Professor West showed up on time, although he looked like he'd made a great effort to do so. His brown corduroy jacket was rumpled and he looked like he hadn't trimmed his beard in a couple of days. "Probably sleeps on a cot in his office," Bella Porter whispered in Sandy Brosben's ear.

Professor West cleared his throat, "You in the flowery, taffeta blouse," he said, looking straight at Bella and reading her name tag. "Bella, let's hear your story first." Bella was caught off guard as she looked around the tiny classroom. All eyes were fastened on her. "Come on up. Don't be shy. I want to see what you're made of."

"I bet," Sandy whispered to Jane Stanley, who was smart enough to ignore her.

"And you're next," Professor West said sharply, pointing the pointer at Sandy Brosben, and tapping it on her desk for emphasis.

Life is Unfair
by Bella Porter

My life has not been easy. Bert and I were newlyweds when Bert got drafted by the army and sent overseas. Whenever we could, we talked on the phone about buying a house and starting a family. Then the phone calls abruptly stopped. The bottom fell out of my world when I got the news of Bert's death. I was a widow and only 22 years old. Can you imagine?

After that, I went on a bender that lasted for years and ended up in the Caribbean not knowing how I got there. I took up with a local fisherman named Beany on account of how he wore his knit hat all rolled up around the ears. After a while, the smell of fish day in and day out got to me and I threw Beany back in the sea. Catch and release. Then I travelled to Europe where I found myself.

Sometimes you have to lose yourself to find yourself. Even grief runs its course. It wasn't how I wanted to define myself. I have beautiful memories to hang on to.

Bella Porter stuck her chin up in the air, challenging anyone who dared to judge her. Then she quietly took her seat.

Chapter 12

Professor West's divining rod woke everyone up from their reverie. It was Sandy Brosben's turn next, and she humbly took her place at the podium.

The Missus
by Sandy Brosben

What does a bored housewife have to talk about, you might wonder? Well, sometimes I'd get up early and bake a batch of oatmeal and chocolate chip cookies and put them in those big, rectangular Tupperware containers they used to make and go visiting. I'd visit shut-ins and soup kitchens and give out my cookies. Just seeing people smile made my day. You should try it.

At other times, I'd get adventurous and add different things to that crescent roll pastry dough they sell at the supermarket—like bits of salami or bacon and cheese. I'd sell my baked goods for Bingo money.

Once I got into a fitness kick after I gained weight doing all that catering and baking. I signed up for yoga classes 6 days of the week—mornings and afternoons. There I was running all over town with my little pink yoga mat tucked under my arm, wearing matching pink spandex.

I'm either never bored or completely bored. Go figure. There's no in-between with me. But that doesn't mean I'm unstable. When I'm bored, I read and sometimes I read on the treadmill. I think that's why I need bifocals. Say, has anybody seen my reading glasses?

Chapter 13

Jane Stanley looked like she was trying to hide in plain sight as she slid down in her chair. Professor West put on his glasses and looked around the room. Jane would have to wait. Let her squirm a bit. "Peter Carmichael? Peter? Your card says you are looking to meet people in therapy. Is that right, Peter?"

"You've taken me out of context," Peter began.

"Whatever," Professor West said dismissively. "Which do you prefer, meeting people or therapy?"

"I never really thought about it."

"Oh, very well, let's have it, Peter," the Professor said impatiently, savoring the moment. Peter looked at the class, and then down at his notes. He'd have to wing it because he'd taken a sleeping pill after supper the previous night and forgotten about the assignment until this morning.

Peter was proud of his power point presentation. He could hear his therapist's voice in his head. *Find your happy place.* He looked at his audience and pictured them naked. He smiled, then caught himself smiling and promptly stopped smiling. He frowned. Then he spoke:

Unglued

by Peter Carmichael

- Why therapy
- Meeting people
- Most beautiful person
- Why take creative writing?

I'm taking therapy because I feel sad and cry a lot. I was born with only one emotion—sadness.

I like to meet people so I forget to feel sad. But when I meet sad people I feel like I'm in love so I am in therapy because I am a relationship addict. It's a vicious cycle. It's complicated.

The most beautiful person I ever met was Raquel Welch. Actually, I didn't really meet her, but I saw her on the boob tube. My therapist says I have tunnel vision. Who am I to argue?

I signed up for creative writing because I doodle too much. Mostly breasts. Large breasts. My therapist said that this class might help break me of this destructive behavior.

If I could become a writer, writer and therapist would become one. Generation versus stagnation. It's classic. Words are going to glue me back together. Come to my book signing. My ego's not done with me yet.

Chapter 14

Professor West was completely enthralled by Peter's presentation. "Wow! Wasn't that a wow experience? Absolutely brilliant, Peter. A hard act to follow. Now it's your turn, Alex. Let's see what this self-proclaimed, unemployed genius has to say for himself."

Living the Dream
by Alex Remington

I am Alex…Alex Remington…unemployed. Now you might say to yourself that I can't hold a job, but it takes a real genius to quit a job and take up writing. I'm winging it. I'm living the dream. Just try to stop me.

I was born to write. There in my crib, I was not reaching to tear off my diaper to let the chocolate nuggets fall out. I was reaching for the word *cah-cah*, and with my *cah-cah* did I not write flowery letters on the wall? It was a sign. Yes, little Alex Remington, not even out of diapers, without formal training, learning to write *cah-cah* in *cah-cah*. Self-taught.

I have a lengthy last name in case you hadn't noticed. Imagine a kindergarten-aged boy who can spell *Remington*. When people hear my last name, they duck. Go figure. Just call me Alex. Alex will do.

Chapter 15

"Bravo!" Professor West exclaimed enthusiastically. "Mary Anne, you're next."

Dino's Diner

by Mary Anne Tiski

Dear folks. I always try to bring you refills, but Dino says I have to get the food out first. Sorry. We're short-staffed. When you order breakfast, don't order one egg sunny side up and one egg over easy. I had a nightmare once that the eggs were winking at me, so after that you get what you get.

I may not be the sweetest dish, but I'm your waitress and Dino's Diner has the best meatloaf in Glendale County. You are all welcome to come into Dino's afterward. The pies are home baked by Maybelline herself. The mincemeat pie served with ice cream is especially delicious, but don't take my word for it. Oh, and by the way—Wendy's little girl is having her birthday soon. She's going to be 6 years old. Can you imagine? Keep that in mind when you leave Wendy a tip. I don't know what else to write. I'm new at this writing stuff. So, I think I'll wrap it up for now. My mother's gone to bed and is snoring in the next room. I'm pretty tired myself. Nighty night.

Chapter 16

"Very tasteful," Professor West said. "You don't mince words. Now for Jane Stanley. Don't be bashful, Jane."

The Typewriter
by Jane Stanley

Before I retired, I was an office clerk at Glendale City Hall. I wrote. I typed. I took dictation and made coffee. I filed. Maybe you had a parking ticket or an overdue bill? I was the one to see. I was the *post it* queen. Pick up dry cleaning. Post it. Doctor's appointment. Post it. Mail goes out today. Post it. Who told you I painted my toenails while sitting on the can? I got the job after high school and it was the only job I've ever wanted. Come to think of it, it was the only job I've ever had.

I learned how to type while looking at a drawing of a typewriter with fingers on it. My fingers are fat, but my fat fingers could move very fast when I had a deadline. My hemline was no more than three inches above the knee. I believe in standards.

"How very refreshing, Jane." Professor West turned to face the class, "See you all next week. Same time. Same place. Be there or be square."

What an odd class, Mary Anne thought, but she felt oddly exhilarated like a whole new world had just opened up for her.

Chapter 17

Al was busy putting in a flower bed around Maybelline's trailer—zinnias, petunias, and marigolds—whatever was on sale. Last year, he planted hollyhocks around the side steps. "Less grass to mow," he chuckled to himself.

It was early May. *A little frost will weed out the ones that aren't going to make it anyway* was Al's rationale. Sure, he didn't have a green thumb, but nobody seemed to notice or care.

Maybelline came out of her trailer and gazed up at the sky. "It looks like it's a good day to paint those driveway rocks." There were rocks along each side of her driveway that came from the gravel pit near Bullhead Narrows. Every other rock was painted red and every other rock was painted white just like the colors of the Canadian flag. But the red paint had faded to pink and the white rocks had turned a sickly yellow. Handy Al would take care of it.

Al loved painting. Rumor had it that one summer he paid some juvenile delinquents to graffiti Bella Porter's house just so he could paint over it. But Bella, being Bella, didn't seem to mind all the attention. Come to think of it, it took him all summer long to paint that one wall. That was the summer when Maybelline and Al were on the *outsies*. Ever since then, whenever Maybelline would run into Bella at the supermarket, she'd give her the evil eye.

Chapter 18

Bella was suspected to have slept with both Maybelline and Marjorie's old men, and no doubt countless others. No respect. In fact, that was what forged Maybelline and Marjorie's friendship—revenge. They say that Hell hath no fury like a woman scorned and, in Glendale County, women like Bella had Hell to pay, at least that's what the preacher preached every Sunday to a packed church—adultery. After the Sermon, the folks of Glendale County were more than willing to fork over their money for the collection plate as the preacher's wife, Delores, dabbed the corners of her eyes with a tissue. "Hallelujah, sweet Jesus," she would say as if she, too, had been the victim of Bella's adulterous ways.

Maybelline and Marjorie talked on the telephone constantly about how they were going to fix Bella's clock. "Bella Porter has used that grieving widow line for over two decades now—"

"—and she's divided Glendale County into two camps—the churched versus the unchurched hypocrites," Erno said, cutting Marjorie off. He grabbed a beer from the fridge. "How can we get mad at a grieving widow? I mean, it's not our place to judge."

"Did you fuck her?" Marjorie asked, grabbing a can of beer for herself. It didn't seem like the first one either, judging by her tone of voice. Erno had no place to hide, no place to go—but wait!—there was Al's.

He dialed his friend's phone number like it was his lifeline, or 911. "Al, you there? Marjorie's having one of her spells again. Mind if I come over?"

"Sure." Erno grabbed his coat and reached for the door handle.

"Bye, sweetie," he said as a frying pan flew past his head. It narrowly missed him and hit the door frame instead. Wood splinters flew everywhere. *One thing is for sure*, Erno thought, as he hightailed it over to Al's. *Al Critch will never be out of work.*

Chapter 19

Al lived three doors down. There was Maybelline's, the Periwinkles, and then Al's little trailer. It was mint green and surrounded by quack grass and dandelions. There was a sign on the screen door, "Come around back." In the back was an old hut with a horseshoe over the latched door and a sign that read, in bold letters, The Doghouse—Men Only.

Inside, Al was half-drunk. He passed Erno a beer from his bar fridge. The Doghouse was rigged with an old stereo. Soon Jake ('Reverend') Periwinkle and Alex Remington showed up, uninvited. A motley bunch. Alex popped open a beer and put the rest in the bar fridge.

"Go home, Reverend. You don't belong here. Go home to your wife," Erno scolded.

"You heard him," Al said. "Erno and I have business to discuss. Private business. And you too, Remington." The Reverend shook his head and left without saying goodbye.

"Does this business of yours have anything to do with the talk of the town?" Remington said, standing his ground.

"It's none of your business. You're worse than a woman, always poking your nose into other people's business where it doesn't belong."

"What's that supposed to mean?"

"It means you weren't invited. Now scram," Erno said, moving a step forward and staring him down. Remington went to the bar fridge to get his beer.

"The beer stays, but you have to go," Al said, defending his turf. "Get your sorry ass out of here! Now!" Al Critch was small, but he'd been a street fighter in his day. Finally, Remington backed down and put his hands up. "Take it easy, man. Alright, alright, I'm leaving. But I just came to tell you that rumor has it that Maybelline bought a gun on the black market and has it hidden somewhere in her trailer. Why do you think she doesn't go anywhere? Because she's afraid somebody's going to break in and steal it."

"If that were true, Marjorie would know and Marjorie doesn't keep anything from me."

Remington ignored Erno and looked directly at Al. "Be careful. Women are unpredictable, especially when they're fixing to settle a score." He opened the latch and let himself out into the crisp night air, not bothering to close the latch. The door of the Doghouse banged back and forth…

Chapter 20

Al and Erno drank in silence, listening to the stereo and Cassie Cassum's Top Hits of the Seventies Countdown. Al reached into a cabinet drawer and took out a joint, then lit it. "You and I need to talk," Al said. "If Maybelline's becoming unglued, why haven't I noticed?"

"You're asking the wrong question," Erno said. "The question you should be asking is why Maybelline's not coming unglued."

"Go on," Al prompted, leaning forward.

Erno took a drag off the joint and exhaled slowly. Al waited patiently. "I'll tell you why," Erno continued. "It's either because she's over your adultery, or because she's got something up her sleeve. Either way," Erno said, poking Al Critch in the chest several times for emphasis, "it's up to you to find the gun before she goes ahead with whatever she's planning to do with it." And he emphasized 'it'. There was a long pause which seemed to go on forever. Then Al spat on the dirt floor. Erno seconded the motion. The meeting was over. There was nothing more to say.

The damage to the door frame from the flying frying pan was minimal due to a key holder which took the brunt of it. Erno had somehow smuggled himself back inside the yellow trailer without waking Marjorie who had fallen asleep at the kitchen table. Several empty Budweiser cans lay scattered on the table and a few had toppled over. Marjorie held a cigarette in her yellowed fingers over a full ashtray and the ash on it was the length of the cigarette. How she managed to sleep and hang onto the cigarette at the same time escaped Erno. *Must be genetics*, he thought. He carried her into the bedroom and put her to bed.

Chapter 21

The next morning, Erno was sitting at the kitchen table reading the Glendale Herald when Marjorie shuffled in and sat down. Her curlers had been removed and the resulting curls had been twisted into a statuesque bun on top of her head. "Good morning," he said softly.

"Good morning," Marjorie replied absently. As was her ritual, she stuck four slices of bread in the toaster and took out the raspberry jam. Just then the door opened. It was Al coming for his morning coffee and newspaper.

"What are you two looking so sober for? Did the cat eat the canary?" Al asked.

"You should know," Marjorie said stiffly. "You're the one who's dating the Cat Lady."

"Which reminds me," Erno interjected, but Al was pantomiming for him to shut up and keep quiet.

"What were you going to say, Erno?" Marjorie asked. "Or do I have to drag it out of you?" The room fell silent. You could have heard a pin drop. Marjorie slammed her cup down hard on the table and glared at the two of them. "Remington came by last night stirring up shit about Maybelline. Says she bought a gun on the black market. Is that what you've been hiding from me?"

"Remington told us the same thing, but we didn't believe it," Erno said. "I mean, you'd think Maybelline would have told you herself if it were true, you being best friends and all."

Mary Anne came into the kitchen wrapping her housecoat around herself. Her hair was a mess and she hadn't brushed it yet. "What's that you're saying about Maybelline?" she asked, yawning simultaneously.

Marjorie looked down at her hands as if looking for answers there. Finally, she blurted out, "Remington's going around telling everyone that Maybelline bought a gun on the black market."

"Nonsense," Mary Anne said, sounding skeptical. "But even if it were true, how would Remington know? If you ask me, Remington's got a screw loose."

Al looked thoughtful, and poured himself another cup of coffee before speaking. "I agree. We can't go around making wild accusations based on hearsay. You know how folks in Glendale county get all worked up. We need something more concrete than Remington shooting off his mouth."

"You've got a point," Erno said. "Got any ideas because I'm fresh out."

"We should flat out ask Maybelline if she recently bought a gun," Mary Anne suggested, "because guns and kids don't mix. She's sitting for Belinda Jane, Wendy Stump's little one. Heaven forbid, what if Belinda Jane were to find it? What if she pointed it at someone thinking it was a toy gun? I'd feel responsible because I'm the one who got Maybelline the babysitting job in the first place."

"Would she even admit to having a gun?" Marjorie asked, pushing away her half-eaten toast.

"I could go over there and poke around," Al volunteered, grasping at straws.

"And I could invite Maybelline over here while you search her place. You still have a key, don't you?" Marjorie asked.

"Marjorie, who do you think you are, the Secret Police?" Erno asked and got up and went to the fridge for his hangover beer. He popped the top and took a large swig.

Chapter 22

"Call her now," Erno urged. "Tell her that Al and me have gone fishing and invite her over for coffee. Then as soon as Maybelline shows up here, call me," Al said, masterminding their impromptu plan of action.

"As the world turns," Mary Anne mumbled to herself on her way to the bathroom to get ready for work.

"All right," Marjorie said reluctantly. As soon as Erno and Al left, Marjorie lifted the receiver. "Say, Maybelline. Erno and Al have gone fishing. How'd you like to come over and keep me company?"

"I've got some pies to bake."

"Can't it wait?"

"I suppose so."

"Great. I'll put on some coffee."

"Give me five minutes."

Marjorie put the dirty dishes in the dishwasher and made another pot of coffee. Soon there was a knock on the screen door and Maybelline stood on the other side of it, proudly holding an apple pie. "Come in. Just set it on the counter," Marjorie said distractedly, stalling for time. "Just a minute while I call the hairdressers to see if there's a cancellation. Maybe they can take me before Friday." She picked up the receiver and dialed Maybelline's number. "Jane, can you fit me in earlier?"

Al was on the other end of the line. "We're in!" he said, and then hung up.

Chapter 23

Al was careful not to let the tomcats out when they stepped inside the tiny trailer. He turned to Erno and said, "I'll check the bedroom and kitchen and you check the living room and bathroom." They began to fan out and go through drawers and closets. Forty-five minutes went by. "It's got to be here somewhere," Al said.

"Yeah, but where?" Erno replied, sounding exasperated. "We've looked everywhere." Suddenly, Al looked up at the ledge over the kitchen cupboards.

"Are you thinking what I'm thinking?" Al asked.

"You bet," Erno replied. Al pulled a ladder up to the kitchen counter and climbed up on it. "Careful. What do you see?"

"A whole lot of dust and mice droppings."

"Keep looking."

"There's a cookie jar shaped like a honey bear. Either Maybelline is trying to lose weight or she's got something stashed up there," Al said excitedly, unsure what to do next.

"Don't just stand there," Erno snapped impatiently. "Open the damn thing!" Obediently, though reluctantly, Al reached up and removed the lid of the cookie jar and reached inside…

Chapter 24

Professor West was happy. The class showed up on time and there were no dropouts. In fact, there was a new addition to the class—Al Critch.

"Welcome to our cozy creative writing class," Professor West said to Al enthusiastically. "Let's just cut to the chase and share what you've written. I presume you didn't come here empty handed," he added offhandedly. Al Critch shrugged and went to the front of the class. He faced his captive audience and cleared his voice:

The Cookie Jar
by Al Critch

My life as a handyman has had its ups and downs. Climbing the ladder of success can be challenging. Once I spilled a bucket of blue paint all over Bella Porter's new white shag carpet. Another time I fell off the ladder cleaning out the Periwinkles' eavestroughs. I've managed to squirrel a little money aside for a rainy day, but I'm old and I don't know how much longer I can keep being a handyman. So I've been buying lottery tickets and putting them in my cookie jar.

Al leaned forward on the podium and gave Remington a hard look, if looks could kill.

"It seems that I'm not the only one with a cookie jar." Al took his handyman's hammer out and, like a judge with a gavel, pounded it on the podium a couple of times for emphasis before returning to his seat.

"That was a nice touch. Very creative," Professor West commented. "See you all back here next week."

When Mary Anne got home, Marjorie asked how the creative writing course was going. She told her mother about Al's story.

"And do you believe Al?" Marjorie asked. "Do you believe the cookie jar is full of money and lottery tickets or do you think it's full of cookies?"

"I think there's more than one cookie jar, depending on who you talk to," Erno said, throwing in his own two cents.

"There you go with your conspiracy theories again," Marjorie scolded.

Mary Anne took off her cardigan and draped it over the back of a chair. Then she set her purse on the table and plopped herself down. "Fools make fun of fools," Mary Anne said. "It's cheap entertainment. We believe our own bullshit because we have nothing better to believe in."

Chapter 25

Al Critch did not believe Remington's story about the gun. He truly did not believe that Maybelline was capable of buying a gun to kill Bella Porter in cold blood out of jealousy because he had slept with the grieving widow. And because he did not believe it, nobody else would either because people looked up to him. Yet just because nobody believed Remington's story, didn't mean it wasn't true.

If all hell was going to break loose, Al Critch was not going to stand in the way. He was going to let Maybelline sort herself out one way or another. Al loved Maybelline more than heaven and hell and everything in between. And that is what that old cookie jar way up over Maybelline's kitchen cupboards signified. It was a prayer, a metaphor. *Don't let me down. I'm nothing, can't you see?* He looked up at the constellation in the Heavens and suddenly he knew exactly what to do. He grabbed the hammer out of his side pocket and he threw it away.

Chapter 26

Saturday night was poker night in the back room of Dino's Diner. One memorable Saturday night, Keystone fronted Remington $50 grand for a game of high stakes poker. It was mid-summer, and the crickets could be heard through the open window. "Jiminy Cricket!" Remington cried out as he raked in money hand over fist. Remington was on a winning streak, and he walked away from the tables with a duffel bag full of cash. Nobody knew that Remington had won money at the illegal gambling tables at the back of Dino's diner except a handful of men who'd lost their shirt that night and they weren't about to sing.

The next day, however, Remington's winning streak came to an end when his trailer caught on fire. Then he conveniently disappeared. Detective Joe Willis knew that something was suspicious, but he just didn't know what that something was. "Give me time," he mumbled, as he wrapped his trench coat more tightly around himself and chewed on a toothpick. Then he spat out the toothpick and pulled out a Cuban cigar. "Some things are hard to quit," he said, blowing smoke rings into the air. "And I'm no quitter," he prophesized smugly.

Chapter 27

"He'll turn up with another scheme up his sleeve," Bella Porter said to the girls at the Dollhouse. "Last year Remington ran for mayor. What'll it be next? Money laundering?"

"You watch too much TV," Marjorie said sarcastically. "I'd say he eloped with one of Keystone's dames."

"Remington was a degenerate gambler," Sandy Brosben pointed out. "His disappearance could have something to do with that." Sandy took a thoughtful sip of her lady's drink and set it down, stopping only to swat a nervy mosquito that landed on her cheek. It was filled with blood, so the resulting effect was much akin to war paint carelessly applied. "And what about his trailer mysteriously catching on fire," Sandy continued. "Coincidence? I doubt it. I'd say that Keystone is behind it and the motive is revenge."

"And then there is the matter of the smoking gun," Marjorie said, lighting her cigarillo and stubbing it out again immediately afterward. "Trying to quit," she said in way of apology.

"Let's just say Remington's bag of tricks might be bigger than we've given him credit for," Marjorie said cheekily, tongue in cheek. The floodgates were now opened wide as conspiracy theories about Remington's smoking gun flew back and forth like a manic badminton game from the twilight zone.

"The pieces fit," Bella Porter sighed as if she'd seen it all before. She got up to replenish their cocktails. "The trouble is there are too many pieces." If Remington was smart, the Dollhouse ladies collectively would outsmart him.

Chapter 28

Marjorie returned from the Dollhouse looking like something the cat dragged in. Erno didn't look much better. "Change your shirt," Marjorie ordered, tossing him a clean one. "That one's got stains down the front of it."

"Nag, nag, nag. Don't you have something better to do?"

"Actually, the Dollhouse ladies came up with a theory about Remington's disappearance," Marjorie said enthusiastically. When she was finished, Erno shook his head.

"I'll be a monkey's uncle," he said at last. "I think Remington was trying to alibi himself the night he came over to the Doghouse talking about Maybelline having a gun."

"What are you saying?" Marjorie asked, hanging on Erno's every word.

"What I'm saying," Erno said. "Is that the day Remington invited himself over to the Doghouse was likely the day he pulled a robbery. I'd say it's Remington who owns a gun, not Maybelline."

"Are you saying that Remington did a robbery to repay Keystone but once Remington had the money he changed his mind and decided to keep it? And then he went and stashed the gun to clear himself and frame Maybelline? But why would he do that?"

"I'll tell you why. Because Maybelline would turn around and blame Al Critch because he's the only one who goes in and out of her trailer that she knows of. Can you see it now?"

"We've got to find that gun," Marjorie said decisively, "before somebody gets hurt."

Chapter 29

Al Critch sat in the Doghouse alone. The kerosene lantern lit up the small shack and cast eerie shadows on the walls. He lit a joint and took a cold one from the bar fridge. Then he reached into the pocket of his coveralls and removed the gun. He turned it over in his hands.

"I never thought Maybelline was capable of this," he said to nobody in particular. That night when Erno and Al had snuck into Maybelline's trailer, Al had felt the gun under the wad of money in the cookie jar, but only showed Erno the money. They had decided to put the money back because it belonged to Maybelline. Then they had left the trailer together and parted ways. But later on, Al had snuck back into Maybelline's trailer and removed the gun.

Now as he sat alone in the comfort of the Doghouse surrounded by a cloud of smoke, feeling omniscient and clear-minded, almost zen-like, Al Critch thought about what he would do next. *Nothing. He would do nothing. He would hear nothing. And even if he heard something, he would say nothing.* And with that Al Critch removed a floor board under his cot and hid the gun. Then he turned off the kerosene lantern and lay down and fell into a deep sleep. If love was blind, Al Critch was certainly that.

Chapter 30

Mary Anne looked at Professor West's business card. She studied the address: 9 Valley View Drive, Apt. 101, Glendale. She got out a map and looked for Valley View Drive. It was only four blocks from the college. She looked at her watch. The time was 8:30 pm. She put the truck in drive and peeled out of the trailer park. Half an hour later, she turned onto Valley View Drive, her heart racing with anticipation. She was tingling all over. What she was expecting to find or do, she didn't know.

Just then a white Oldsmobile sped past heading toward Valley View Drive too. It pulled in behind an apartment. Mary Anne followed and watched as a woman stepped out of the car. She couldn't believe her eyes. It was Jane Stanley! By the flush on her face, it looked like she'd been doing a lot more than just typing!

The next morning at Dino's, Nancy Gilmoss brought news about the mysterious Professor West. "I managed to talk the Head librarian into letting me look at class yearbooks in Archives," Nancy said proudly. "It turns out that there was a *Horatio* West who attended Glendale Elementary in the early forties. That must be your notorious Professor West. Nobody by the last name of West has attended Glendale Elementary since then." Nancy smiled sympathetically, placing a warm, weathered hand over Mary Anne's.

On the drive back to the Silver Fox Trailer Park, Mary Anne felt like she was in a trance. She kept checking the cars that drove past, hoping to spot the elusive Professor. The thought of going for a drive together, just the two of them, sent thrills up and down her spine. But suddenly jealousy crept into her fantasy world with thoughts of Jane Stanley and Professor West making out. Mary Anne drove on in silence, and then decided to pull into the parking lot of the Liquor Mart. She bought a six pack for herself and a 12-pack for Erno and Marjorie to fight over.

"Haven't seen you in a while," Tom Jenkins said as she paid for the booze. "Tips at Dino's must be pretty good from the looks of all that change," Tom commented chattily. Mary Anne smiled sheepishly. "By the way, how's that creative writing class going?" Tom asked as an afterthought.

"What do you mean by that?" Mary Anne asked, feeling paranoid. *If put on the spot always answer a question with a question. It'll bide you a little time.* Mary Anne fished Professor Horatio West's business card out of her purse and handing it to Tom. "Here, ask him yourself."

"You don't have to get all huffy about it," Tom said, feigning hurt feelings.

"Must be menopause," Frank Smith said from somewhere in the lineup.

"Too young." Della Scott volunteered from the next aisle.

"Maybe she's pregnant," Tom said, his tone conspiratorial.

"Nah, if she were pregnant, she wouldn't be buying liquor," Frank Smith said wisely.

"Maybe she has a hot date," Della Scott piped up again, putting a bottle of sherry on the counter.

"She is the hot date," Tom Jenkins chuckled. "Problem is the little lady's so hot that nobody has the courage to 'man up' if you get my drift?" Frank Smith started to laugh, but Della Scott gave him the stink eye. "Will that be all, Della?" Tom asked, sounding like a perfect gentleman once again.

Della rolled her eyes. "Men," she said, as if that explained everything.

Chapter 31

Back at the trailer, Mary Anne took off her cardigan and plopped herself down. "Liquid supper," she said, opening a beer and putting the rest in the fridge. "Help yourself," she volunteered, feeling generous. "Cheers!"

"Maybelline called," Marjorie piped up. "She said your Chevy was spotted on Valley View Drive. It didn't take long for the patrons at Dino's to figure out what that meant," Marjorie added smugly, a sly smile appearing on her made up face.

"I was just taking a drive. Last time I checked, it wasn't a crime," Mary Anne said defensively, taking a swig of beer.

"Since when does my daughter just go for a drive?" Marjorie asked.

"Since she's been taking that creative writing course," Erno said with a smirk.

"Oh, that's it! Mary Anne is practicing her creative driving skills," Marjorie added.

"Say, doesn't the Professor live on Valley View Drive? Where's that business card?" Marjorie asked, reaching for Mary Anne's purse.

"Mother, don't you have something better to do like redo your curls?"

"Ouch!" Marjorie exclaimed, feigning hurt feelings.

"Ouch back!" Mary Anne replied, and then added, "Truce." For the rest of the evening, they pigged out on day old subs from Dino's and played 3-handed cribbage. The stakes were low, and their moods were high. The Professor Pied Piper can wait, Mary Anne thought. If he was going to be chased by every eligible woman in town, she'd sit this one out over and over again expecting to get the same results. She was not crazy, she decided. Or was she? Decided or undecided aside, one thing was definitely for sure, and that was that the idea of dating a man she'd never even dated was far more intimidating to her than going all the way.

Chapter 32

Alex Remington just had the best and worst day of his life all rolled into one. It started in the afterhours club in back of Dino's Diner. He'd sat down at the high stakes poker table and that was when the trouble began. Keystone was sitting at the table, a Cuban cigar stuck between his teeth. He was wearing a white fedora tilted rakishly and wearing a long, white cashmere coat. Rumor had it that Keystone had his finger in every black-market pie there was. At the moment, he looked more like a pimp than a poker player with young vixens draping themselves all over him. But it was all part of the ruse because the babes made it look like keystone had a good hand when he had a lousy hand and vice versa by the expression on their faces and their oohing and aahing.

"Shut up, Bunny, and you too April. Can't you see I'm in the middle of a poker game? Go powder your nose or something." Keystone brushed imaginary lint from his coat. "Your turn, Frank."

"I fold," Frank said.

"What about you, Remington?" Keystone asked, laying his cigar in the ashtray and taking a shot of whiskey.

"I say that Bunny and Honey are coming home with me," Remington said confidently.

"April," Keystone corrected. "Bunny and April, and they're not part of the deal."

"What deal?" Frank asked. Keystone ignored him.

"Are you going to play or not?" Keystone snapped impatiently.

"You know what?" Remington said even more confidently. He pushed all of his poker chips toward the center of the table. "I'm feeling lucky tonight. All in."

"Are you sure you want to do that?" Keystone asked.

"Oh, I'm sure alright."

"Okay, but it's your funeral," Keystone replied. "Better pick your pallbearers while the picking's good," he added with a chuckle, followed by a whiskey chaser.

Chapter 33

Detective Joe Willis turned off the tape recorder. Keystone Federno sat across from him in the interrogation room down at the precinct. "You threatened him," Detective Joe Willis pointed out. "Not a very good alibi, especially for a pro like you."

"But I'm telling the truth. You can even ask Frank Smith. He was at the poker table too."

"Don't worry, Keystone. I've only just started my investigation. Don't leave town."

Keystone put his head in his hands looking like a broken man. "What am I going to tell Laura and the kids?" he began. "We were going to take a family trip to Disneyland."

"You'll just have to find him before I do," the Detective said sarcastically. "And I suggest you get yourself a good lawyer. You'll need one."

Chapter 34

Thomas loved his job at the casino. He loved the action and he made enough money from the lucky gamblers to live off his tips. It just so happened that Thomas lived on Valley View Drive too, and although all he saw when he looked out his living room window was a strip mall, he didn't mind. What he did mind, however, was his meddlesome neighbor across the hallway, Jane Stanley. Jane was forever making excuses to knock on his door. First it was to borrow a hammer to hang pictures. Then it was sugar for her coffee. Finally, even mild-mannered Thomas had had enough. He was going to have to put his foot down, but how or when this event was going to take place, he just didn't know.

"What gives?" Mary Anne asked as she slid onto a bar stool.

"Ever have a neighbor who knocks on your door a little too often?" Thomas asked.

Mary Anne wrinkled her nose and scrunched her eyes hard, trying to remember. "Nope," she said and popped a maraschino cherry into her mouth and fiddled with the toothpick before tossing it aside. "I'll have another one of these. More Shirley, less Temple," she said playfully.

"I must have missed that class in Bartending School," Thomas replied, adjusting his bowtie.

Mary Anne leaned forward conspiratorially, "Could you put half a shot of Jack Daniels in it, you know, to take the edge off?"

"What will I do with the other half shot?"

"I'm sure you'll think of something."

Thomas told Mary Anne about the cougar across the hallway. "Any advice?"

"If I were in your shoes, which I'm not," Mary Anne began, feeling suddenly important and wise, "I would confront her."

"I've been thinking the same thing, but how? I don't want to hurt her feelings."

"Why don't you play matchmaker, you know, set her up on a blind date." Mary Anne rummaged around in her purse for Al's business card. "Ah, there it is," she said when she found it. "Pass me the phone." Thomas promptly did as he was told and Mary Anne dialed Al's number. She explained the situation.

Al was more than eager to be of assistance. "Women like that always need something fixed," he said before hanging up. Mary Anne passed Al's card to Thomas who squinted as he read it. *Al Critch, handyman. Can fix anything. No job too big or too small.* Followed by the phone number.

"Just slip it under her door, and good luck," Mary Anne said, grinning from ear to ear.

"What do you mean good luck?" Marjorie asked, taking a seat beside her daughter.

Mary Anne ignored her. Marjorie opened her glittery clutch purse. It was full of $20 bills. She winked. "Nothing like a hard day's work."

"What will it be?" Thomas asked.

"Nothing tonight. It's getting late. Take me home, Mary Anne."

Chapter 35

Mary Anne filled up the gas tank before heading home. As she pulled into the Silver Fox trailer park, Marjorie suddenly let out a scream and covered her mouth, pointing. An ambulance was parked outside their yellow trailer, lights flashing. Maybelline was standing outside. When she saw them, she rushed over to the chevy. Mary Anne reached over to the passenger side and rolled down the window. "Erno called 911 and then called me," Maybelline said, sounding frantic. "I came right over. He had a heart attack. The paramedics are working on him now. Oh, Marjorie. I'm so sorry."

Marjorie quickly got down from the truck. In her haste, she forgot to wait for the step stool and fell flat on her face. She struggled to get up and hobbled up the front steps. "Erno! Erno! Hang in there!"

"Stand back, ma'am!" one of the paramedics ordered. "I've just given him the paddles and a shot of morphine. He's stable for now, but we've got to get him to the hospital."

"I'm coming with you," Marjorie exclaimed. A small crowd had gathered around the ambulance as Erno was carried out on a stretcher.

"Is he dead?" Reverend Periwinkle asked.

"If he were, his head would be covered with a white sheet," Mrs. Periwinkle replied, apparently an expert on such matters.

"What happened?" Al asked.

"Heart attack," Maybelline replied.

"Poor soul," Bella Porter said sympathetically.

"Alright, rubberneckers. Scram!" Mary Anne ordered, shooing them away. She went inside and closed the screen door. It was quiet. Too quiet. Just then the phone rang. She wondered who it could be at this late hour. She picked up the receiver. It was Keystone, Erno's brother.

"Is Erno there?"

"He's on his way to the hospital. Didn't you hear?"

"Hear what?" Keystone asked.

"Erno had a heart attack. They don't know if he's going to make it or not. They had to restart his heart."

"Shit!" Keystone shouted into the receiver. Mary Anne could hear noise and people talking in the background.

"What's this about?" she asked.

"I'm a suspect in Alex Remington's disappearance. Detective Joe Willis told me not to leave town."

"What have you gotten yourself mixed up in? We're practically family, Keystone. Come over and I'll put on a pot of coffee."

"Look Virgin Mary Anne. Just tell Laura if she calls looking for me that I've left town."

"I thought you two split up."

"We hit a rough patch."

"Why can't you call her yourself?"

"Can't. Phone's probably bugged."

"Where are you calling from?" Mary Anne practically shouted into the phone, as if doing so would drown out the noise on the other end of the line.

"Dino's."

"At least tell me where you're going, so I can let Erno know if he pulls through."

"Bullhead Narrows. There's a motel and a bar up that way. Look Mary Anne. I gotta at least try to find Remington. I was counting on that $50 grand I lent him so I could take Laura and the kids to Disneyland."

"You lent Remington $50 grand? What? Are you out of your mind?" Mary Anne asked incredulously. There was a click at the other end of the line. Keystone had hung up. "Nut job!" Mary Anne yelled into the receiver before hanging up too. She couldn't decide what type of con man her uncle was, but calling Erno? What for? And why now? Erno didn't have much money and the brothers weren't close. So it had to be something else. She opened the door to the trailer and stepped out onto the porch. The moon was full and she could make out the Big Dipper and the North Star. She took a deep breath. *Let sleeping dogs lie.*

Chapter 36

Maybelline returned to her trailer and reappeared a short time later with her two tomcats. Their leashes had somehow gotten tangled and she was trying to untangle them when she looked up and saw Mary Anne.

"Erno's going to be alright," Maybelline said reassuringly. Mary Anne nodded silently. She wrapped her cardigan more tightly around herself. Maybelline picked up Tyler and Mary Anne walked down the trailer steps to scratch the tomcat between the ears.

"Keystone called," Mary Anne said, a worried look on her face.

"What'd he want?"

"To speak to Erno."

Maybelline looked down at the ground and kicking at a clod of dirt.

"He's headed to Bullhead Narrows to look for Remington. I don't like the sounds of it," Mary Anne added.

"Me neither. Why don't we drive up there and do some sniffing around ourselves?"

"Sure, why not? Mother can call a taxi when she's ready to come home from the hospital."

"Alright. I'll just take Earle and Tyler back to the trailer and grab a sweater."

Soon the old Chevy turned onto the highway and was headed east toward Bullhead Narrows. Mary Anne had a million things on her mind—Erno's heart attack, Marjorie, Dino's Diner, her creative writing class, Professor West, the list goes on. She looked over at Maybelline. Maybelline squeezed her hand.

"He'll pull through," Maybelline said soothingly. "Don't you worry your pretty little head," she said as she rearranged her brassiere.

"It's not me I'm worried about," Mary Anne replied, hitting a pothole and cursing. "It's Mother. She's got bad nerves."

Maybelline nodding sagely, sympathetically. They passed row upon row of cookie cutter houses that all looked the same except for the landscaping. Some yards were landscaped with shrubs and small trees while others had flowerbeds bordered with white rocks. Still other yards were bare except for swing sets and children's toys scattered around. Parents could be seen sitting in lawn chairs minding their children as they played or firing up a barbeque.

"You know, there's a whole other world out there," Maybelline said, turning to Mary Anne. Then she pointed excitedly.

"There it is, the Sundance Saloon!"

"Where?"

"Over to your right." Thursday was barbecued ribs night—two racks of ribs for the price of one. The place was jammed packed.

"Hungry?" Maybelline asked.

"Starved."

Chapter 37

Mary Anne parked the Chevy and they went inside. The bar was dimly lit. Red and white gingham tablecloths and matching curtains gave the place a cozy atmosphere. Most of the tables were full of diners who were chowing down on ribs and sharing a pitcher of draft beer.

A hostess wearing a gingham pinafore that matched the tablecloths greeted them at the door. "Hi! My name is Heidi," she said, flashing a smile and showing off her good dental hygiene. "Table for two?" Mary Anne nodded and soon they were seated at a deuce by the window. Maybelline looked around the saloon and saw a tall, lean man bellied up to the bar eating peanuts. *I'll bet that's his supper*, Maybelline thought compassionately, unsure if he was Remington or not. She nodded in the thin man's direction.

"I'm going to the ladies' room," she said which was code for "going to get a closer look."

"Careful," Mary Anne mouthed, and Maybelline winked as she wrestled her plump body out of the chair. She started to make a beeline for the peanut bowl, but decided against it. *Too obvious. I'll take a closer look on the way back*, she decided.

Feeling impatient, and running on adrenaline, Mary Anne went over to the bar and asked for a soda water. The thin man at the counter turned to look at her.

"Do I know you?" he asked, sounding genuine.

"I was going to ask you the same thing," Mary Anne replied, dipping into the peanut bowl.

"Charles," the thin man said, extending his hand.

"Charmed," Mary Anne said demurely, squeezing Charles' hand daintily. "And does Charles have a last name?"

"Remington. Charles Remington," the thin man said.

Mary Anne had just taken a swallow of soda water and suddenly started choking upon hearing the name. She struggled to regain her composure. "I've got to get back to my table. I hear the ribs are pretty good."

"See you round," Charles said, grinning foolishly.

Mary Anne returned to her table and joined Maybelline who was already gnawing greedily on ribs. "These are delicious," Maybelline said, licking her fingers. "Have some before they're all gone." Mary Anne picked up a rack of ribs and tried to decide the most delicate way to eat it. Finally, she gave up and let her stomach decide, feeling like a cave woman as she pulled the meat off the bones.

In no time, music from the local band made them almost forget the reason they were there. The lead guitarist and vocalist sang a tune from the Beach Boys about California girls. He bopped his head to the beat of the music, sending his bleach blonde, shoulder-length hair flying all around his face. Mary Anne filled Maybelline in about Charles Remington as the waitress came to take away their plates and bring their bill.

"My treat," Mary Anne said, picking up the tab. "Keep the change," she said to the waitress. Then Mary Anne turned to Maybelline and leaned forward, "Let's head to the truck. Maybe we can find out where Charles Remington lives."

Chapter 38

Once outside, Mary Anne turned to Maybelline. "Are you thinking what I'm thinking?"

"That Alex Remington might be hiding out at Charles' place here in Bullhead Narrows?"

"That's right," Mary Anne said matter-of-factly, as if she had it all figured out. "I have an idea. We'll follow Charles home."

"How are we going to do that without being noticed?" Maybelline asked, genuinely perplexed.

Mary Anne leaned forward conspiratorially. "We'll follow him home and I'll flash the lights when he pulls into his driveway. Then I'll roll down the window and tell him his tail light is out." "Wait!" Mary Anne said excitedly. "Here he comes now!" Charles Remington strolled nonchalantly out of the bar holding a beer. He took a swig and set the bottle on the roof of his black, beat up Ford. It was half full. Charles belched and slid in behind the wheel.

"What a loser," Maybelline said, smiling at Charles. Charles smiled back and revved the truck's engine before peeling out of the parking lot. Gravel spit out from behind his rear tires and the beer bottle rolled off the roof and smashed when it hit the ground. Mary Anne pulled in behind him as smooth as molasses.

"Piece of cake," she said.

"Are you always this happy when you're up to no good?"

"Absolutely," Mary Anne replied with a smug look of satisfaction.

Charles drove along the side streets of the quaint little town. He turned off his headlights like a well-practiced drunk driver. Finally, he turned into a long, narrow driveway flanked by cedar hedges. The house was dark, except for a porch light that was surrounded by flies and moths. Mary Anne pulled in behind the Ford, and flashed her lights a couple of times.

"Shit!" Charles said, thinking it was the local cops. He stopped and Mary Anne stopped too. She turned off her headlights and stepped out of the Chevy.

"Hey!" Mary Anne said, trying to sound casual. She stuffed her hands into the back pockets of her jeans, a non-threatening posture she'd learned about in a dating magazine.

"Hey back!" Charles replied. "Wassup?" he slurred.

"Do you always drive with your headlights off?" Mary Anne asked, walking around Charles' truck inspecting the dents and cheap, backyard body work.

Charles ignored her and took a swig of beer. "Want one?" he asked, diverting the conversation.

"Aren't you even going to invite us in?" Mary Anne asked coyly.

"Mary Anne!" Maybelline exclaimed under her breath, not sure if this was a good idea. Then Maybelline turned to Charles. "I have to get up early," she said, lying through her teeth.

"Yeah, the place is a mess. I wasn't expecting company anyway," Charles said apologetically. Just then a light in the front room went on and a face briefly appeared in the window before disappearing behind the curtain again. Mary Anne looked at Maybelline and Maybelline looked at Mary Anne. They both couldn't have an overactive imagination at the same time. Or could they?

Chapter 39

"I'd bet money that it was Alex Remington you saw in the window," Bella Porter said to Maybelline, taking a sip of her cocktail. The Dollhouse ladies were circled around Maybelline, anxious to hear more. Maybelline felt like a movie star being interviewed about her latest movie. She primped her hair and smiled sheepishly.

"What do we do next?" Jane Stanley asked.

"Eyes and ears," Bella Porter replied in a hushed voice and the Dollhouse ladies nodded gravely. "Meeting adjourned!"

"Did Bella raise an eyebrow or did she just tweeze too much that morning?" Marjorie asked herself, but couldn't be sure, so she filed it away for future reference. "En garde!" Marjorie said, pointing her cocktail umbrella menacingly at Bella. It fell defiantly and rolled off the balcony. Everyone in attendance knew enough not to laugh at Marjorie when she was the devil's right hand...

Chapter 40

Marjorie visited Erno daily at Glendale General Hospital and Mary Anne visited after her shift whenever possible.

"I don't know why you are so hung up on that professor," Erno said to Mary Anne. A nurse was taking his blood pressure and had just removed the cuff.

"West. His name is Professor Horatio West, Erno," Mary Anne said, sounding annoyed.

"You should take it easy," Marjorie scolded, squeezing Erno's hand. "Besides, Mary Anne is old enough to make her own decisions." Mary Anne walked over to the window and adjusted the blinds to let in more sunlight.

"We were young once too," Marjorie said, going over to her daughter and pulling her close. Erno took a sip of water from the nightstand next to his bed, mauling over what Marjorie said like it was a new revelation he hadn't considered before.

"Mary Anne, can you run to the store and pick me up a 12-pack? Even this hospital water tastes like medicine."

"I'll see what I can do," Mary Anne said reassuringly, not meaning a word of it.

Alex Remington paced nervously back and forth. Charles had let Alex stay with him in Bullhead Narrows, but only conditionally.

"What have you gotten yourself into now?" Charles asked. "You know two ladies by the names of Mary Anne and Maybelline were at the Sundance Saloon tonight. Seemed out of place. Said they were from Glendale. Ring any bells?"

"Yeah. Plenty. Mary Anne and Maybelline live in the Silver Fox trailer park. In fact, the two are neighbors. Mary Anne works at Dino's Diner and Maybelline bakes their pies and muffins."

"They followed me home. Caught me driving without my headlights. Very *Keystone* if you ask me," Charles said.

"Keystone?" Alex asked, panic-stricken. "What about Keystone?"

"I mean like Keystone cops, cop Wanabees."

"Oh," Alex replied, recovering his composure, then added, "I saw them in the driveway."

"Well if you saw them, they must have seen you too," Charles said, sounding irritated. "I won't be harboring no fugitive, even if he is my half-wit brother, do you hear me?"

"I'll pack my shit in the morning and clear out," Alex promised, hanging his head.

"You can't keep running. Whatever you've done, it can't be that bad."

"They were leaning on me."

"Who's they?" Charles asked, leaning across the kitchen table.

"Keystone and his goons. I owe them big time."

"Tell them you don't have it."

"I wish it were that simple. Keystone said he is going to personally castrate me if I don't come up with the money. He staked me 50 grand for a game of high stakes poker."

"He what? How could you be so stupid?"

"I need time to think," Alex pleaded.

"Alright, I suppose you are entitled to one good hangover on me. There's beer in the fridge, but you're sleeping in the bathroom. There's a window you can crawl out of if the shit hits the fan. And it probably will…"

Chapter 41

It was late September and sandals with socks weather. Nobody rolled their eyes at you in Glendale County for making a fashion faux pas. And why not? Because if it was rainy, all you had to do was wring out your socks, not change your soakers.

"Trying to make a fashion statement?" Erno asked from his hospital bed as Al walked into the room wearing socks and sandals.

Erno was sitting up in bed sipping on a Chocolate Boost. "Hey, Dumb Ass, how's it going?" Al asked sincerely. "Nurses treating you well?"

"They don't wear skirts anymore. Can't see where to pinch," Erno replied, taking another sip of Boost. "I could use a beer right about now to take the edge off." Just then Marjorie stormed into the room, shooting Al a stern look. She gave Erno a peck on the cheek.

"No beer for a while. Doctor's orders," Marjorie scolded, forever the mother hen.

"Say," Al said, changing the subject, "did you hear from Keystone?"

"Can't say I did," Erno replied, tongue in cheek. "Why?"

"Because he called your house. He's looking for Alex Remington." Erno gave Al a blank look but fidgeted uneasily with his blankets.

"He's not his brother's keeper," Marjorie said sternly, applying some pink frosted lipstick. She dropped the tube in her purse and angrily snapped it shut.

"Stay out of this, Marjorie," Erno warned, raising his voice.

Marjorie gathered up her purse and wrapped her shawl around her arthritic shoulders. "I'm going home," she said quietly and left the room. When she was gone, Al drew closer to Erno's bedside and came eyeball to eyeball with his oldest friend.

"They think Keystone set Remington's trailer on fire because of gambling debts. Of course, this is all speculation."

"He what!" Erno exclaimed adamantly.

"Why'd he try to contact you?" Al Critch asked, leaning forward. "Are you in on it?" he added conspiratorially.

"In on what?" Erno asked, turning red. He rang for the nurse who came rushing into the room. "I need some nitro," Erno said, choking on his words. "And get this clown out of here," he added, pointing a shaky finger at his long-term frenemy. "I'd stick to painting if I were you. This doesn't concern you."

"Whatever you say, pal," Critch said defensively. "Call me when you've come to your senses, will you?"

Alone in the hospital room once again, Erno thought about his brother and none of it made any sense. Keystone was a businessman, but a criminal? No way. He was a family man. He never crossed that line.

That night, Erno tossed and turned but couldn't sleep. He thought about what Critch had said and started worrying. He decided to call Keystone's house.

"He's not here," Laura said. "What's he done, Erno? You're his brother. You should know."

"You're his wife," Erno shot back. "You tell me."

"You've got to find him before he does something crazy if it's not already too late," Laura pleaded.

"I'm in the hospital. Heart attack." Erno said matter-of-factly as if it was routine for him. He paused and took a sip of water from the bed stand. "Go look under a rock. That's where snakes hide," Erno added for emphasis and quietly hung up the phone.

Chapter 42

Keystone Federno checked into the Roadhouse Motel on the outskirts of Bullhead Narrows. He put his luggage down and sat on the edge of the bed. Then Keystone did a strange thing. He wept. Buckets. He couldn't tell the police that Alex Remington had gotten one over on him. And why not? Because in his mind, not only had Remington taken his money with no intention of paying it back, but Remington had torched his own trailer so the cops would blame him for it. Then there was Remington's mysterious disappearance. Circumstantial, yes, but very compelling. And Remington, that bastard, just might get away with it.

Remington couldn't sleep because he had to guard the money he had stashed in his duffel bag and because the bath tub was too God damn short for a good night's sleep. He thought of burying the money but what if he forgot where he'd buried it? And then there was the issue of Keystone. No, he had to skip town. He would hitchhike clear across the country and live off the money. But $180,000 wouldn't go far. He'd have to find a job. He'd have to start fresh without ever looking back and saying goodbye to his friends. But could he do all that? Could he walk away from the cat and mouse game? Who was he fooling hiding out at his brother's house? Logical first place they'd look. Not too bright. Suddenly he began packing a duffel bag full of clothes, not bothering to fold them. He stuffed the wads of money in his gym socks and packed them too. It was 2:00 am and he stank like booze. He left Charles a note:

Leaving for God knows where. Don't call the cops. I'm not missing. I'm going on a permanent vacation. I can never contact you again. Tell Mom and Dad that I'm in the Witness Protection program. Translation: Deep Six. There are rules. They can't protect me if I break the rules. I miss you already.

P.S. Bye. Forever.

He left the note on the back of the toilet and opened the bathroom window and began to crawl out, then changed his mind and crawled back in. He tore up the note and flushed it. Satisfied, he took one last look at himself in the mirror and walked out the front door. He walked to the edge of Bullhead Narrows and stuck out his thumb. The first car that came along stopped and backed up.

"Where're you headed?"

"Easy street."

"Say what?"

"Easy street."

"Where in tarnation is that?"

"Just take me as far as you can go, then drop me off at a coffee shop. A few bucks for a soup and a sandwich would be mighty fine. Mighty fine."

"Anything you say," the farmer said. "Don't mind the company if you don't mind the smell of cow manure."

Chapter 43

Professor West rapped his pointer on the desk. "There is no such thing as a bad book. The closest thing to a bad book is an incomplete book." The class fell silent, taking it all in. "I see we have a missing student," Professor West said, looking at his seating plan. "You are all required to bring a doctor's note if you are sick. You can pass that message along to Mr. Remington."

"I don't think that creative writing is one of his priorities at the current time," Peter Carmichael said.

"Haven't you heard?" Mary Anne blurted out.

"Heard what?"

"That Remington left town. Even his brother hasn't heard from him."

"And his trailer caught on fire," Sandy Brosben pipped up.

"He'll fail the class," Professor West said threateningly. "The final essay is worth 75% of the grade and the title is, Whatever Happened to Alex Remington. Class dismissed!" Then Professor Pied Piper abruptly closed his briefcase, stood up, and marched out of the room with his loyal students, looking both shocked and confused, trailing after him.

Chapter 44

Even if he had to search through the rubble, Al Critch was going to check things out. He pulled into Alex Remington's driveway and stepped out. The yard was overrun by weeds and sawgrass and the screen door, in dire need of repair, was swinging back and forth. Al stepped inside and looked around. Rumors that Remington's trailer had burned to the ground were grossly exaggerated. The fire had been contained to the kitchen, most likely a grease fire. The kitchen cupboards were singed and the paint on the wall beside the stove had been peeled off by the fire. The air was heavy and suffocating so Al opened the window over the kitchen sink to let in some fresh air. He took a glass down from the cupboard and poured himself some water from the tap, reflecting on Professor West's words, *Write about what you know.*

An empty fire extinguisher lay in the middle of the kitchen floor. Al stared at it long and hard. Then an idea came to him. *The question is not who started the fire. The question is who put the fire out?* Alex Remington's truck was still parked outside. "That's odd," Al said to himself and started walking around from room to room. Dresser drawers were pulled out and a suitcase lay on the bed, open but empty. "Where are you?" Al said out loud as if looking to the heavens for an answer. Maybe he decided to take a duffle bag instead. Less conspicuous. Yeah, and maybe he called somebody to pick him up. "Damn it!" Al exclaimed excitedly. "It looks like Alex Remington, that weasel, staged his own disappearance." Everyone knew by now that Keystone had fronted Remington $50,000 for high stakes poker, but nobody thought to ask if Remington had won or not. They just assumed that he lost or else he would have been able to repay Keystone the money. But what if he won money and got greedy and decided to keep it, all of it? That could equally explain his disappearance.

Yeah, he's still out there, Al Critch decided, opening a cookie jar and stealing a couple of ginger snaps. Then he went to the fridge and poured himself a glass of milk, continuing on to the bathroom mirror to inspect his milk mustache. *I can feel it in my bones*, Al added, reaching for some Absorbing Junior in the medicine cabinet and applying it to his shoulders and neck. *He's on the move because he's hit the jackpot*, Al decided as he pulled a bag of weed out of the back of Remington's toilet and started rolling himself a doozy. *Must have lost his mind*, Al thought as he made smoke circles, *because who in their right mind would leave behind a bag of weed this good?*

Al left the screen door flapping back and forth and jumped back in his truck. "Open and shut!" he shouted as he swung his old beater around and headed back home with the bag of weed tucked safely and securely in his glove compartment.

Chapter 45

The further away from Glendale County Alex Remington got, the better off he felt. He rolled down the window and extended his arm, feeling the wind through his fingers. Man, it felt good to be alive.

"Mind if I light up?" the farmer asked.

"Not at all."

"Want one?" not waiting for a reply, the farmer pulled out two reefers from his front pocket, lit them both and passed one to Alex. "Name's Joshua. What's yours?"

"Remington," Alex said, inhaling deeply. "Alex Remington."

"Are you a spy? Like Bond…James Bond?" Joshua asked, feeling suddenly self-conscious.

"No, nothing like that," Alex replied, laughing at the thought.

Joshua looked visibly relieved. "Where are you headed?" Joshua asked, making small talk.

"No man's land."

"Well, you're headed in the wrong direction," Joshua said, shaking his head.

"How do you figure that?"

"Because all the pretty women live over in Cedar Falls north of here. As a matter of fact, there's a dance tonight at the old red barn on the outskirts. What do you say, cowboy? You like pussy, don't you?" Remington laughed and coughed at the same time.

Joshua made a U-turn in the middle of nowhere and pulled over onto the shoulder of the road. "Time for you to get back in the saddle, cowboy, or you'll forget what your woody pecker's for." The farmer chuckled, and stuffed a couple of thick joints in Remington's shirt pocket and winked. "That's for courage," he said with a serious expression on his whiskered face. Remington shook his head and grabbed his duffel bag from the back seat and stepped out onto the shoulder of the road. He waved as Joshua did another U-turn and carried on his way again.

Before too long, a yellow Ford sedan with a woman behind the wheel slowed to a crawl. She gave Remington a hard look before rolling down her window. "Where're you headed?"

"Cedar Falls."

"You don't seem so sure."

"Why do you say that?"

"Hop in." Remington jumped in and slammed the door shut, throwing his duffel bag in the back seat.

"Hi, I'm April."

"And I'm Alex."

April shrugged.

"Thanks for stopping."

"What's in Cedar Falls?" April asked innocently.

"There's a barn dance tonight. I figure I'd check it out."

"Who told you that?" April asked.

"Just some guy who gave me a ride."

"Does this guy have a name?" April pressed.

"Joshua."

"That figures," April said, laughing. "Joshua is a self-appointed match-maker around this neck of the woods. He has five daughters and had them all married off by the time they were 18. But if I were you, I'd go to the Sundance Saloon in Bullhead Narrows. Better prospects."

"I'm just—" Remington was a poor liar.

"Come on!" April said excitedly, and swung the car around. "I'll buy you dinner."

Chapter 46

"Are you asking me for a date?" Alex asked, surprised at how fast his luck was changing.

"As a matter of fact, I am. Say, you look familiar. Have I seen you before?"

"People say that all the time," Alex replied, lying through his teeth. He smiled. His tell. Soon they were pulling into the parking lot of the Sundance Saloon and were seated at the bar.

"Now I remember you," April said, her voice rising. "You're the guy who won all that money gambling. Keystone's looking for you, Alex, and he's mad as hell. Says you owe him big time."

The color drained from Alex's face. *Were customers staring at him or was it his imagination?* "Not so loud," he said under his breath. "I'll have a double," Alex said when the waitress came around. "And the same for my date," he added, emphasizing the word 'date'. He pulled out a couple of $100s and slid one over to April. "You're paying, pretty lady, but I'm getting what you're paying for," he added, adjusting his belt.

April was quick to pick up on his subtleties. She grabbed his belt buckle and pulled him closer. "Do I look like a bounty hunter to you?"

"Wait till we have a few more of these. I haven't quite made my mind up about you," Alex said with a straight face, but the liquor was kicking in. "Cheers!"

"Ride 'em, cowboy!" April giggled, touching her glass against his and lifting it high. Alex began to feel nervous about leaving all that money in the car so he thought up an excuse.

"April, I left my inhaler in the car. I need to get it."

"Okay, sweetheart," April said, batting her eyelashes. She jiggled her car keys in front of him teasingly. "You'll need these. Hurry back."

Chapter 47

Alex took the car keys and kissed April on the cheek. "I will, honey," he said, and winked. The yellow sedan was not hard to spot in the parking lot. If April suspected his windfall was in his duffel bag, she didn't let on. When Alex got to the car, he retrieved the bag from the backseat and rummaged around in it. He could feel the wads of money rolled up in his socks and felt immediately relieved. *I should split*, he thought to himself, *but April was too damned hot.* Then he thought of Keystone. April was Keystone's mistress and that meant she was off limits. Did Keystone's wife Laura know about April? Suddenly it all became crystal clear to Alex what he should do. He should go to Keystone's house and give the $50,000 to Keystone's longsuffering wife. Then he should return to the Sundance Saloon and pick up where he left off. The hell with the rules.

He scrawled a note—*April, I'll be back in one hour. There is something I have to take care of. Alex*—then he walked over to Hank Lapaloosa, the bartender. "See that little lady over there? Give her this note."

"Do it yourself," Hank protested gruffly. "Can't you see that I'm—" Alex slipped him a $100 bill.

"I'll get right on it. Anything you say. I aim to please," Hank said quickly, changing his tune.

The key turned easily in the ignition and soon Alex was on his way back to Glendale. He knew where Keystone lived because Keystone was the richest man in town. Twenty minutes later, he arrived at the millionaire's mansion which was surrounded by hedges and an iron gate. Alex pulled up to the gate and cautiously buzzed the intercom.

"Hello?" Laura answered tentatively.

"Laura, it's Remington. Alex Remington."

"Keystone's not home."

"I have something that might interest you."

"I'm not supposed to open the gate to strangers."

"But I'm not a stranger, Laura. You and my ex-wife went to school together. You remember Anne, don't you?" There was silence at the other end which seemed to last forever. At long last, Laura buzzed open the gate and Alex drove up to the mansion. He counted out $50,000, put it in an envelope, and tucked it in his breast pocket. He was not afraid of returning the $50,000 that Keystone had lent him. But he was afraid that Keystone might sic his goons on him and roll him for the rest of the money which was $130,000 that he had won legitimately despite the gambling establishment being illegal. He couldn't very well go to the police if he got rolled for the rest of the money, and he couldn't keep running either. *Let the chips fall where they may*, Alex thought as he stepped out of the car. Laura was waiting for him at the door. Two Dobermans were growling behind her.

"Lisa, would you take the dogs and put them in the back yard?" Soon a teenage girl in pigtails appeared. "This is my daughter, Lisa." The girl smiled, then disappeared with the dogs. "Won't you come in? I'll put on some coffee. Fresh muffins just came out of the oven too if you'd like some?" Laura added, warming to her visitor.

"I can't stay," Alex said apologetically. He reached into his breast pocket and handed Laura the thick envelope full of money. "I owe your husband money. It's all there. What I owe him. Here, take it." Alex took a deep breath.

Laura took the thick envelope and turned it over in her hands. "You're lucky Keystone's not home," she said crisply. Alex Remington looked down at his shoes, feeling suddenly awkward and unsure of himself. "I think you'd better leave."

"Alright," Alex replied. "I'll take a rain check on the coffee and muffins," he added before getting back in the car. The gate was already open when he reached it and he drove on through without looking back.

That was easier than I thought, Alex said to himself, feeling relieved. But he would have to find a place to stash his money before he returned to the Sundance Saloon, and fast, but where? Then it hit him. He returned to the trailer and cut a hole in his mattress. Then he stuffed the money into it and duct taped over the hole. After this, he took a mattress pad cover out of the linen closet and put this on the mattress and made up the bed as usual with fresh linens and a blanket. Once his handiwork was done he patted the bed, amazed by his own brilliance. Then he locked up the trailer and headed back to the

Sundance, but not before sparking up one of the joints that Joshua had given him. "For courage!" he shouted out loud to the Gods after inhaling deeply. "Nothing like it!"

Chapter 48

Just then a cop car came barreling up behind him flashing its lights, sirens blaring. Alex pulled over. "Fuck! Fuck! Fuck! And fuck!" he shouted, pounding on the steering wheel with his two fists, but the cruiser zoomed past him. "What the fuck? Holy fuck!" Alex exclaimed. "I think my luck's about to change." He continued on to the Sundance Saloon, a penitent man.

"Car thief!" April shouted when he rejoined her. "You had no right!"

"I paid Keystone back every red cent I owed him," Alex replied, catching his breath. "I didn't want to spoil this evening by looking over my shoulder."

"What'd you mean?" April asked, putting out her hand for her car keys. Alex took her hand and kissed it like a chivalrous knight.

"Keys please," April demanded, still sore at him, but softening. Alex plopped the keys into her outstretched hand. "You still never answered my question."

"I think it's obvious that we have chemistry, April. Keystone has a wife. He's not right for you. I want you to be my girl."

"Whoa, Cowboy! Did they teach you that in rodeo school? Why so serious all of a sudden? I'm just a party girl. I thought you were cool with that." She opened her compact and applied some cherry red lipstick.

"Okay party girl. Wanna smoke a joint?" Alex pulled his one remaining joint out of his pocket and rolling it back and forth between his fingers. Then he ran it underneath his nose, inhaling deeply. "This is fucking good stuff."

"Why the hell not?" April asked as Alex led her by the hand and headed for the back door. In the alleyway, a man was pissing up against the wall, his pecker in one hand and a bottle of beer in the other. He looked at April and grinned. "It's not like I haven't seen one of those before," April said, rolling her eyes. Further down a young couple were humping up against the wall. "Now ain't that a sight for sorry eyes," April said, feigning disgust.

"That's sore eyes," Alex corrected.

"Whatever. Gimmee that!" April demanded, grabbing the soggy joint from Alex and sucking on it with her lipstick-smeared lips. "Got a light, mister?" Just then the back door of the Sundance Saloon swung wide open, illuminating the entire alley. Out of the shadows stepped none other than Keystone looking larger than life. He was pointing a gun at April. Alex turned as white as a ghost, then fainted. Keystone stepped over him.

"Don't mind if I do," Keystone said, and pulled the trigger as flames flared up from the novelty shop lighter.

"Fancy meeting you here," April said.

"I could say the same for you," Keystone replied. "Hold that thought. I've got a phone call to make." He went back inside and made a beeline for the payphone beside the bar. He dialed Detective Joe Willis's direct line. "I've found him."

Chapter 49

"Found who, Boy Scout?" Detective Willis asked sarcastically. "Do you know what time it is?"

Keystone ignored that last remark. "Alex Remington, that's who."

"Where are you?"

"I'm at the Sundance."

"Where is Remington right at this very moment?"

"Passed out in the back alley."

"Can you hold him till I get there?"

"I can't promise you that."

"Look, wise guy. I can overlook the illegal gambling but the kitchen fire in Remington's trailer is still under investigation...or do you want to be charged with obstruction of justice?"

"Detective Willis, Keystone is the man for the job!" Keystone said with a whole new attitude. He hung up and headed for the rear exit. The patrons in the bar parted like the Red Sea. You could hear a pin drop. The hardcore rubberneckers headed for the rear exit while the hardcore alcoholics bellied up to the bar.

Keystone knelt down beside Remington and whispered in his ear. "Make this look good you son of a bitch. I have a reputation to protect." He grabbed Alex Remington by the hair and threw him up against the wall. "Spread 'em!" he commanded, and frisked Remington briskly, squeezing his balls.

"What are you trying to do, make lemon aid?" Alex protested, not knowing whether to laugh or cry. Instead, he pissed himself.

"Turn around!" Keystone ordered and Remington obeyed. Keystone pulled out some zip lock ties from his rear pocket. In no time, he had Remington hogtied. "Zip ties," Keystone said, facing the crowd, "are a Keystone's best friend and this," he said, pulling out his fake gun and waving it into the crowd, who promptly ducked. "Anybody have a cigarette?"

"I do!" April said, stepping out of the shadows. She was trembling in her stilettos like a newborn fawn on wobbly legs.

"This is not the time to propose!" Keystone bellowed, taking a cigarette from April. "Go inside everybody. The show's over."

Keystone lit his cigarette and blew a smoke ring, watching it grow bigger and bigger in the light of the street lamp. Then he grabbed April by the waist and walked her back inside. "Hank, April has had too much to drink. Do you mind driving her home?" He took April's car keys out of her purse and handed them over. "And fill her gas tank while you're at it," Keystone said, stuffing a $20 bill into Hank's pocket. "I'll close up."

Keystone called Laura from the bar phone. She answered on the first ring. "I found Remington. He's at the Sundance Saloon and I'm waiting for Detective Joe Willis to show up and take him in for questioning. I don't know when I'll be home." Laura was used to her husband's long hours and coming home late just as long as he called.

"He was here earlier."

"You didn't let him through the gate, did you?"

"I thought it would be alright. I went to school with his ex-wife, Anne. He brought the $50,000 he owed you."

"Did you count it?"

"It's all here. Every penny. Come home."

"I will once Detective Joe Willis gets here."

"And bring me a hamburger and a chocolate shake. These muffins taste like cardboard."

Chapter 50

"Hog-tying a man just ain't right," T-Roy said, noticing that a small crowd had gathered around Remington.

"You're not kidding," Mary-Lynn exclaimed, pulling up her pantyhose, or what was left of them.

"What should we do? We have to do something," T-Roy exclaimed, "but how can we get past that crowd."

"I have an idea," Mary-Lynn said, suddenly inspired. "I'll distract them while you cut the zip ties with your pocket knife."

"Brilliant idea."

"Hey beautiful people, wanna see something?" Mary-Lynn stepped up on a stack of crates. Then she turned around, bent over, and hiked up her skirt.

The small crowd abandoned the hog-tied man and moved toward Mary-Lynn and her little striptease. "More! Show us more!" they shouted. Meanwhile, T-Roy went to work cutting Alex loose. His wrists and ankles were rubbed raw and bleeding.

"Can you walk?" T-Roy asked.

"I think so," Alex responded, struggling to get up.

"Whoever did this to you might come back. If I were you, I'd make myself scarce."

"Here Bud," Alex said, and stuffed a $100 bill into T-Roy's jean jacket pocket. "Get a room."

T-Roy laughed to himself. "Gee, mister. You didn't have to…"

But Alex Remington had already disappeared around the corner. In his haste, he ran into a homeless man pushing a shopping cart full of rattling cans. Then an idea hit him. "I'd like to buy your cart and trade coats." He flashed a $100 bill to prove that he meant business. The homeless man stood there with his mouth open, mesmerized by the money. Remington put the bill into the bum's grubby hand and traded his own coat for the homeless man's knee-length one. "That $100 will buy a lot of booze to keep you warm." The bum gave him a toothless grin.

Soon Remington was pushing the rattling cart down the alley looking every bit the part as he shuffled along like an old man down on his luck. In the distance, he could hear hooting and hollering and "Take it all off". The crowd went hog wild when Mary-Lynn shook her booties at them. At the Five and Dime, he bought himself a steaming cup of coffee.

"You new in town?" the cashier asked. "Hey, wait a minute, ain't that Pete Doyle's coat?" The cashier was a large, middle-aged black woman and her name tag read Myrtle. Myrtle looked like she could take care of herself if push came to shove. She continued, "I gave Pete that coat and you ain't Pete. Give it back!" She came around the counter and started grabbing for it.

Alex took it off and apologized. "I'm not looking for any trouble ma'am. Here, take it." And he walked backward toward the door all the while keeping an eye on the store clerk. He almost walked right into none other than Detective Joe Willis but kept his head down and looked away when the Dick yelled at him to watch where he was going.

"Was that jackass giving you any trouble?" Willis asked Myrtle, paying for a chocolate bar.

"He stole Pete's coat but took it off when I confronted him. I'll take it home and wash it. Pete's probably missing it. He used to go to our church before he joined the army and was shipped overseas. Came back a damaged man," Myrtle said, shaking her head. "Crazy as a loon but gentle as a lion."

"Don't you mean lamb?"

"Are you getting biblical with me?" Myrtle asked, batting her eyelashes and leaning over, showing her ample cleavage.

Detective Joe Willis raised one eyebrow, then headed for the door.

"You forgot your change!" the cashier called after him, and shook her head, smiling to herself.

Detective Joe Willis stood outside the Five and Dime. He peeled back the candy bar wrapper and took a bite. He had a feeling in his gut but he didn't quite know what it was. He took another bite from his chocolate bar and threw the rest away. *Homeless people need to eat too*, he thought as he headed for his car.

Chapter 51

Keystone polished off his beer and went outside to check on Remington, but when he opened the back door, he saw that his prisoner had vanished. He was still reeling when Detective Joe Willis tapped him on the shoulder. "Okay Wise Guy, where's Remington?"

"He's gone."

"He's what?"

"I don't know. One minute I had him hogtied and the next minute—poof! Gone!"

"I should have known better than to trust you. Next time I need a favor, I'll call a real cop."

"You do that."

"I could use a drink," Detective Joe Willis demanded, slapping his hand on the counter impatiently.

"The bar's closed," Keystone said matter-of-factly.

"Then re-open it."

"No can do. Hank's cashed out and the money's locked up in the safe."

"In that case, how about a double scotch on the house?"

"I don't think you should be drinking when you're driving the cherry-mobile, Copper, but I could get you a Shirley Temple," Keystone said, smirking. He started getting out the grenadine and a glass. After he made the non-alcohol beverage, he garnished it with a nice, plump cherry and pushed his fait accompli toward Willis.

Willis shook his head, and popped the cherry in his mouth. "Nice little joint here. See much action except back alley humpers?"

"I wouldn't know," Keystone said, looking bored. "I'm only here because April called. She's the one who led me to Alex Remington."

"Where could he have gone?"

"I think he's run out of game. I'd say he's gone back home to fix what's left of his trailer."

"Yeah, yeah, yeah. I'll swing by there," Joe Willis said nonchalantly, finishing his drink and tossing his ice cubes into the peanut bowl. "I wouldn't eat the peanuts if I were you," he added. "There're disgusting."

Chapter 52

The sun was coming up and Alex hadn't slept a wink. He had stolen a blanket from a clothesline and wrapped it around himself like a shawl as he sat in the alley behind the Sundance Saloon. He never imagined life would hand him such a mixed bag of tricks. Which did he prefer, having more brains than money or having more money than brains? He took a final swig of coffee and was about to toss out the cup when a lady of the night wearing a long fur coat and stilettos, and not much else, sashayed up to him. Her eyes were glazed over and her mascara was smeared. Then she did a surprising thing. She reached down in her bra and produced a crumpled $10 bill which she tossed in Alex's empty coffee cup.

"Say, what the—"

"Bet that got your attention, didn't it, honey?" Alex got to his feet and introduced himself.

"And I'm Bunny."

"Something tells me that's not your real name."

"If brains were money, you'd be dangerous, Wise Ass."

"How much?"

"That depends."

"I mean for the coat. I'm really in a bind."

"Say, wasn't that you I saw hog-tied in this very same alley last night?"

"I can explain—" Alex began.

"—Save it!" Bunny snapped, snapping her bubble gum. "Time is money, and I'm on the clock. Why should I sell my fur coat to you?"

Alex looked down at the ground. Then he looked Bunny in the eye. "Because I'm good for it."

"Say Alex. Have a light?" Bunny asked, pulling out a long, slender cigarillo. Alex lit it for her. "Give me one good reason why I should believe you," Bunny demanded, blowing a smoke ring over Alex's head.

"I'll give you ten good reasons," Alex said and retrieved the crumpled, soggy $10 bill from his coffee cup and stuffed it back down Bunny's bra.

"Wise Ass."

"Do we have a deal?"

"Alright, alright," Bunny said, feigning annoyance. She took off her coat slowly. "It's fake anyway." Alex reached for the faux jaguar coat. "Not so fast, cowboy. I live over the mini mart. You still owe me." Alex Remington was about to ask Bunny how she figured on that when Bunny put her finger to her mouth and sucked on it like it was a popsicle. Alex turned a thousand shades of red and his mind went blank. "Let's just say that you look like you could use a friend. If you need a safe place to hide out for a while, just ask Myrtle to let you into the apartment. You have met Myrtle, haven't you?"

"Yeah, and she's scary."

Bunny smiled knowingly. "It's just her façade. Hard on the outside, soft on the inside. She's good people. Say, where do you live anyway?"

"The Silver Fox trailer park."

"Out in Glendale County?"

"Yeah, you know it?"

"I grew up there. I got pregnant and moved away to live with my aunt Stella in Toronto. Unwed. That's the way things were done back in the day. But enough about me. How're you getting home?"

"I'll hoof it to the highway and then stick out my thumb. In this faux jaguar coat, I'll be the star attraction. Cars will slow down to get a better look." Alex looked at the coat with growing admiration.

"Yeah, the coat does kind of makes you look like Mick Jagger. Good luck *Mick Jagger*," Bunny purred, blowing smoke circles over his head.

What a lady, Alex thought as he walked out of the back alley and joined up with the real world. He felt like Alice in Wonderland. The question was whether or not he was out of the rabbit hole. Only time would tell. Or Bunny, for that matter. He gave Myrtle a broken smile as he abandoned Pete's shopping cart full of rattling cans and bottles in front of the Five and Dime.

"Hey, you can't leave that thing here!" Myrtle shouted when she caught sight of the shopping cart. "Come back here right this minute!" Alex shrugged apologetically and carried on his journey, not sure if he had a comfort zone anymore. Not that it mattered.

Chapter 53

Alex got a lift straight to Glendale by Stella, a kind-hearted silver-haired lady who dropped him off at Marjorie and Erno's doorstep. "Thanks for the ride. What do I owe you?" Alex asked when he got out of the car.

"Your company was good enough," Stella replied, "but you could throw in the cougar coat for free if you like."

"It's a jaguar—oh, never mind. Alright. It's a deal." And he stripped out of the coat and laid it reverently across the backseat.

"That coat's going to bring me luck. I can feel it in my bones," Stella exclaimed triumphantly, "and it sure ain't arthritis."

"Hey, that looks like Alex Remington," Al Critch said, looking out the trailer window. "What's he doing here?" Without waiting for a reply, the handyman opened the door and in marched Alex who made a beeline for the coffee pot.

"I didn't know my coffee was so good," Marjorie quipped. I should start charging a dollar a cup. "Aren't you even going to say hello?"

"Hello Dolly," Alex said and gave Marjorie a squeeze and a peck on the cheek. "I'm looking for Al. My trailer needs to be repaired ASAP or it'll be condemned."

"There are rumors that you robbed a bank. Is it true?" Marjorie asked.

"Marjorie!" Erno scolded.

"Who's going around saying that?"

"People talk, Alex, in case you hadn't noticed," Mary Anne said. "First you go on about Maybelline having a gun and then you disappear. Folks at the coffee shop think it's your gun and you did a robbery with it."

"That's ridiculous!" Remington said, raising his voice.

"Why'd you take off then? You have an essay for the creative writing class that's due on Monday and it's worth 75% of your grade. Professor West is steamed. He even made the next essay assignment about you, entitled, *Whatever Happened to Alex Remington?*"

"That's outrageous!" Remington said, looking visibly shaken. He sat down slowly. "I took off because I owed Keystone money. He has a reputation in case you've forgotten. But I paid him back. Every red cent. I swear. And now I need to see about getting my trailer fixed because there was a kitchen fire." He turned to Al Critch. "Name your price."

"I was over to your trailer yesterday and yeah, it looks bad. How much did you win minus Keystone's cut?" Al said, hoping that his intuition was correct.

"Never mind how much. Is $15,000 enough?"

"Thirty."

"Ten. Take it or leave it," Remington said, standing up, holding his ground.

"Deal," Al said, putting his empty coffee mug in the sink. Erno grunted from the couch. Marjorie was not sure if he was grunting from his triple bypass surgery or because Mr. Fix It had just agreed to repair Alex's trailer for a measly $10,000.

"Why so cheap?" Marjorie asked.

"Because Al fixed my plumbing once and saved my bag of weed, not to mention my sorry ass." Remington explained.

"Which reminds me," Al said, handing over the baggie of weed. "I was holding this for you."

"You stole my weed," Remington protested, half-seriously.

"I was just keeping an eye on your trailer while you were gone."

Remington let it slide. He was not in a position to argue. "When can you start?"

"Right away. We'll head over to the hardware store and pick up some supplies, then round up some guys from the trailer park. You'll have to front me half for supplies."

Arrangements were made and soon hammering could be heard from across the trailer park. Young boys stood with their mothers watching the men work, imagining what it would be like to be big enough to fix things that needed fixing. Later that afternoon, Maybelline came by with a picnic hamper filled with cold cut ham sandwiches and cans of Pepsi.

Chapter 54

They hammered and sawed and hammered again using floodlights after the sun went down. When they were done, they lit some joints and sat on the floor in the sweet-smelling sawdust and wood shavings. Al produced some cold beer from a cooler in his truck and the men toasted to a job well done.

"You know, this place looks even better than it did before the kitchen fire," Remington exclaimed, counting out the rest of the money for the job. "You deserve every penny of it." He took a swig of beer and a drag from his joint. "And what I realized when I was gone is that I couldn't leave this place even if I wanted to. Glendale County is all I've ever known and I belong here."

"You aren't getting mushy on us?" Reverend Periwinkle asked with a wink. Alex winked back.

Peter Carmichael asked if he could spray paint something on the walls like 'Glendale Rocks' but Al Critch poked him in the ribs. "Save it Peter, that's so not cool. Alex, you have to write an essay about what happened to you. You talk and we'll get Jane Stanley over here to type it up so you don't fail the class. Go ahead, call her." Alex did just that and, even though it was one o'clock in the morning, Jane Stanley pulled up in her white Oldsmobile. In she walked with her portable typewriter and set it on the table. Alex Remington sat across from her. All eyes turned to Alex, who began—

Whatever Happened to Alex Remington?
(That's me)

I won money gambling, but I owed $50,000 to Keystone who fronted me money. I was afraid Keystone would get greedy and take all my money, so I holed up in my trailer and got high and drunk. Then I cooked some fried chicken and must have blacked out. I woke up terrified, smelling smoke. I thought someone was trying to kill me and burn me alive. I put some of the fire out and called 911. Then I bolted. The fire fighters must have come and put out the rest of the fire.

After that, I hitched a ride to Bullhead Narrows and almost made it to Cedar Falls, but turned around and ended up at the Sundance Saloon where Keystone caught up to me. Keystone hog-tied me in the back alley, but two lovebirds spotted me and cut me loose. The thing was that I had given Keystone's wife, Laura the money but Keystone didn't know it yet. In all honesty though, I don't think it was all about the money for him. Keystone was getting a charge out of humiliating me.

When I came to my senses, it all felt like a bad dream. That is when I knew I had to get back to the trailer. Make amends. Fix it. Start over.

Jane Stanley pulled the last page out of her typewriter and set it on top of the others. Then she closed her typewriter, stood up, and took a deep breath. "I think you'll be okay now," she said. "You're among friends."

Chapter 55

Alex Remington sat restlessly in his chair in the back row of Professor West's creative writing class. Professor West had read his essay and addressed the class. "It seems that our prodigal son has returned to the fold." Alex had been growing his hair out and it was braided in a dozen tiny braids and colorful beads compliments of Myrtle. The Professor looked directly at Alex over the top of his reading glasses. "Hog-tied?" he asked mockingly.

"You said to write about what you know," Alex replied defensively, feeling like he was in Kangaroo court.

"Okay, wise ass, tell me what you know about hog-tying." Professor West paced back and forth in front of the class, obviously enjoying the theatrics.

"I, um…" Alex began, then quickly regained his composure, "I don't know anything about hog-tying because I'm not a pig farmer, but I do know what it feels like to be hog-tied."

"What you're saying is that you know what it feels like to be a pig!" Professor West shot back. The entire class burst out laughing, even modest Jane Stanley, who covered her mouth with her hand.

Alex turned beet red but held his ground. In fact, he stood up, straight and tall, and marched to the front of the classroom. Turning around, he hoisted his chin in the air like it was the national flag, his beaded braids swinging wildly, matching the crazed look in his eyes. "You know what I mean, Professor. Why are you bullying me?"

"You missed two of my classes. No doctor's note. You could have at least called."

"I had extenuating circumstances."

"I'll say, Houdini, but your essay seems incomplete."

"How so?" Alex replied, still standing.

"You said you wanted to start over, but you didn't explain how you are going to fix your life."

"As I recall, the essay topic was supposed to be about what happened to me and I nailed it. I didn't say how I'm going to fix my life because that wasn't part of the assignment." Alex returned to his seat, apparently done explaining himself.

"He's right," Jane said, coming to Alex's defense.

"Aren't you a little hard on him?" Bella Porter added sympathetically. "He could have post-traumatic stress."

"Do you have post-traumatic stress?" Professor West asked Alex, using his pointer to move Alex's beaded braids out of his eyes.

Alex suddenly jumped up, grabbed the pointer and cracked it over his knee. "No!" he shouted, "but I'd sure feel a whole lot better cutting you a new one." The entire class laughed again, but this time it wasn't Alex they were laughing at but Professor West. "What's wrong?" Alex continued, "it's suddenly not funny anymore when the joke's on you?"

Professor West promptly got up. "Your grades will be posted outside the classroom in a week's time." Then he did a curious thing. He took a wad of chewing gum out of his mouth, stuck it on his desk and marched out of the room. No one followed.

Chapter 56

Alex walked up to the podium and leaned on it. He looked out at his captive audience. "Don't be fooled," he began. "This has to be about more than creative writing. This has to be about each and every one of you. You matter, and together we're strong. But the way I see it," Alex continued, "is that Professor West is a big phony. If he wants you to make something of yourselves, then why does he shoot you down? I'll tell you why," he said, running his fingers through his beaded braids as if fishing for secrets there, "because he wants you to think you are nothing without him." Alex walked over to Mary Anne and looked her straight in the eye. "The truth, so help me God, is that you will become somebody again as soon as you let go of the ties that bind. Enough is enough!"

"Enough!" the class shouted back.

"I can't hear you!" Alex said encouraging.

The class began chanting. "Enough! Enough! Enough!"

"That's quite enough!" Alex shouted. "We need to teach that *prick* a lesson he'll never forget because it's unethical to let a bully decide your fate. Kind of strips you of your dignity, don't you think?"

"What do you suggest?" Bella Porter asked, overcome by curiosity.

Alex turned to Al Critch. "You're Mr. Fix it. How would you go about fixing Professor West's clock?"

"Oh, I don't know—"

"—Tick! Tock! Tick! Tock!" Alex said impatiently.

"Amen!" The class shouted in unison, sounding more like a spiritual revival than a band of co-conspirators.

"I've got an idea," Al Critch said suddenly, leaning forward. The class got out of their seats and circled around him.

"What is it?" Jane Stanley asked excitedly. Her fingers were twitching as if she wanted to type the minutes of the class session word for word.

"We'll arrange for him to meet Honey, a known prostitute. Mary Anne, you have the Professor wrapped around your pretty little finger. Call him and arrange a farewell bash. Do it! Now!"

Mary Anne hesitated and hung her head. She was not sure which way to turn.

"Mary Anne, Professor West was never a nice guy. You made him into someone you needed him to be. 'Hey lady! I don't have all day!' Ring a bell?" Peter Carmichael asked.

"How did you—"

"—I was in the next car at the red light. Remember? He honked his horn and shouted at you and suddenly you're in love. I think you need to see a shrink."

"Is that how you see me?" Mary Anne asked, sinking down in her seat.

"He's right," Sandy Brosben said softly. "Professor West gave you a little attention even though it was the wrong kind of attention, and suddenly you're hooked."

"I hate to break it to you," Bella Porter said, offering her two cents, "but Professor West is only capable of being in love with himself. If I were you I'd think twice about being his doormat."

"Listen to her," Jane Stanley said, "if anyone knows men, it's Bella."

"What's that supposed to mean?"

"I'm just trying to help Mary Anne come to her senses. We all are."

"Are you ready to make that phone call now, Mary Anne?" Al Critch prompted, handing her the receiver. "Tell Professor West to meet you at the Sundance Saloon next Saturday." He dialed the number on the Professor's business card.

"Hello?" Professor West answered, picking up on the first ring. "Who's this?"

"It's Mary Anne. Meet me at the Sundance Saloon this Saturday. Come and take what's rightfully yours." Ever so gently, she replaced the receiver in the cradle.

Jane Stanley giggled like a schoolgirl. "Where on God's green earth did you ever learn to lie like that?"

"You go girl!" Bella Porter whooped.

"This is better than therapy," Peter Carmichael said. "Wait till I tell my shrink."

"You don't need to tell your shrink," Alex Remington said, "she already knows about the plan."

"She does?"

"Peter, you're so gullible, it's pathetic," Alex said, "but sure, why not, come along. Bring your shrink. Whatever. Meanwhile, I'll contact Honey and set it up."

"What have I gotten myself into?" Mary Anne asked aloud, beginning to have self-doubts.

"Look here," Alex said gently, "that magical bubble of yours has got to burst and this is going to help you grow up."

"Revenge?"

"It's either that or have diminished mental capacity for the rest of your life…choose…pick a side…"

"Mary Anne, all you have to do is show up," Al Critch said, helping Remington out. "You can always duck out early. The rest of us can keep the drinks flowing. The prick won't even notice you're gone," Al added, trying to console Mary Anne but having the opposite effect.

"Alright then. We all know what we have to do," Alex Remington said, closing his satchel. Peter Carmichael looked confused, and Alex spelled it out for him. "We need to teach dear old Professor Horatio West a lesson in humility." And with that, their new hippy messiah got up and headed for the door.

"Mysterious ways," Jane Stanley said, gripping her portable typewriter like it was a brief case. "Mysterious ways."

Chapter 57

Joline Honey Smith was thirty-two years old and street-wise. She moved to Bullhead Narrows after she did a five-year stint for manslaughter at the Women's Correctional Facility in Cedar Falls. She was fully paroled. Her crime? Stabbing her ex-husband to death in a drunken, jealous rage when he came home smelling like perfume and pussy. She didn't like men. But she sure loved to fuck them. And it was in prison where she met a prostitute who had killed her pimp. *Trixie's* lawyer used the Battered Woman defense. Trixie taught Joline *the ropes* and Joline came out of prison a reformed woman. She was, in every sense of the word, a professional. She gave men what they wanted—a blow job, straight sex, or ass. The sex was free but her clients were asked to donate money to fund her charity work 'up front please'. One of her clients was a lawyer named Carl Withers who taught her how to stay out of trouble. She paid for Carl's services in exchange for free sex and there were rumors that Carl Withers was operating as Honey's pimp. Business was booming.

Early the following day, Alex Remington and Al Critch turned up on Honey's doorstep. After hearing their sale's pitch, she promptly told them, "You'll have to get somebody else. I run a clean business and I don't get involved in anything that smells of scandal. Now if you don't mind, I have somewhere I need to be."

"But we were counting on you."

"I said no."

"It's because of Carl Withers, isn't it?"

Honey proceeded to shoo them toward the door. "Carl's got nothing to do with it."

"Everyone has a price. What's yours?"

"I'm not in the business of setting people up. Now take a hike!" Honey added, getting angrier by the minute.

"Okay, okay, just thought I'd ask," Alex said, passing Honey a crisp $50 bill. "It's to fund your 'Save the Jaguars' campaign." Honey gave him a phony smile and slammed the door in their faces.

Critch looked at Remington and Remington looked at Critch. "We have three days to come up with a plan before Saturday night or our plan falls through," Al Critch said.

"Yeah," Alex Remington replied, "looks like we're back to square one."

Chapter 58

Saturday night came sooner than expected and Alex Remington decided to *wing it* without Honey's help or blessing. Mary Anne wore her party dress made of sparkling sequins and matching stilettos. Then she picked up Maybelline and they headed for Bullhead Narrows.

"You look stunning!" Maybelline said, eyeing Mary Anne's dress and shapely figure. "Professor West would be crazy not to fall for you."

"Who said anything about—"

"You know Mary Anne, Alex and Al just want to get Professor West drunk to see his true colors. Think of them like your big brothers looking out for you. I mean, if he turns out to be a real jerk you can write him off before the first date. That's the whole point to 'the plan'."

"You mean it's not all about revenge and teaching the Professor a lesson?"

"No, of course not, sweetie. There, there," Maybelline said sympathetically.

"And what about saying that I have diminished mental capacity and that I need to humiliate Professor West to grow up?" Mary Anne sobbed.

"That isn't exactly what they said. You're twisting their words."

"Am I? Well then could you please explain to me what this is all about because quite frankly I don't know."

"You have a lot of friends in Glendale County who don't want to see you get hurt. We need to know if dear old Professor West is hard on the outside but soft on the inside or a real jerk through and through."

The drive took only half an hour and before long they saw shimmering lights up ahead. The parking lot of the Sundance was packed. A flashing neon sign advertised Happy Hour and the daily Specials, along with the weekend entertainment. The tangerine sun was beginning to set. Mary Anne pulled into the parking lot and put the Chevy in park.

"Come on kiddo, your friends are all waiting for you."

Maybelline began to open the door but Mary Anne grabbed her arm. "Wait!" Mary Anne said, sounding frantic. "What about the prostitute they were going to set him up with? How do you think that makes me feel?"

"You know have men are. That was just 'man talk'. They weren't really going to go through with it." Maybelline leaned over and whispered seductively in Mary Anne's ear, "'Come and take what's rightfully yours.' Those are your words, not mine, remember? You led Professor Horatio West on so he's counting on you to deliver, baby." Maybelline stepped out of the truck and straightened her skirt. "Are you coming or not?"

Mary Anne sat in the truck for a few minutes trying to gather her courage. "What have I gotten myself into?" she asked herself and wondered if she was the only person alive who felt so conflicted. Finally, Mary Anne stepped out of the Chevy, side-stepping a pile of vomit as if it was her rite of passage to do so.

Chapter 59

Maybelline joined up with the others at a long table consisting of several tables pushed together. "Look who's sitting at the bar," Maybelline exclaimed, taking a seat beside Bella Porter and ordering a margarita.

"You don't say," Bella said. "Apparently Professor West doesn't like our company."

"And he won't let us buy him drinks either," Sandy Brosben piped up. "Look!" Mary Anne had joined Professor West at the bar and was eating from the same bowl of peanuts. "How romantic," Sandy cooed.

"We have to put a stop to this!" Remington protested.

"Wait!" Al Critch ordered. "Let's see what's going to happen next. We can always stage an intervention." He nudged Remington and winked. Everyone at the table laughed.

Peter and his shrink were having a friendly game of pool over in the corner of the bar by the vending machine. "Peter's such a show off," Bella said, sounding disgusted. "And look at his shrink touching him on the shoulders encouragingly. She's old enough to be his mother. If you ask me, it's borderline incestuous."

"Cradle robber!" Bella shouted in their direction.

"Tramp!" Peter shouted back and his shrink whispered something in his ear and then grabbed his hand like an overprotective mother and made a beeline for the door.

"Where do you think they're going so fast?" Al asked. Alex just shook his head, his beaded braids bouncing about his face.

"What can I get you, Mary Anne?" Hank Lapaloosa asked politely. Did she detect a slight smirk on his face? She wondered. Maybe she was being a little paranoid.

"I'm driving. I can't drink."

"The Sundance Saloon offers free rides home. Keys please."

"What do you take me for?"

"It's not negotiable. And you too Romeo," the bartender said, referring to the Professor. "You can't have a good time in a bar drinking pop or coffee." Without further coaxing, they threw their keys into a big bowl which the bartender kept behind the counter.

"Car thief!" Professor West yelled and Mary Anne laughed.

"Okay," Mary Anne replied, "I'll have a rum and coke. Light on the ice."

"Same here," the Professor said, "come on, let's have a game of pool."

"What? I can't—"

"—It's not negotiable," Professor West said, heading to the nearest table and racking them up. "Let's see who scratches first."

By midnight, Remington, Critch, and Maybelline were up on stage singing 'Stray Cat Strut'. All three laced their arms together like they were paper dolls, totally oblivious to why they had come there in the first place. In the morning, it would dawn on them, but right now they were having way too much fun.

Chapter 60

After a few shots of liquid courage, Mary Anne tried some fancy bank shots but ended up sinking the black ball. "I can't do this anymore. I'm a lousy shot."

"I'll give you points for honesty," Professor West said laughing, and took a seat at a corner table.

"Last call for alcohol!" Hank Lapaloosa shouted and Professor West went up and got them two more rum and cokes. Hank dimmed the lights when April got up on stage and began singing, "They call it a trap…I can't walk out…because I love you too much baby."

"Al Critch and Remington lured you here to set you up with a prostitute," Mary Anne suddenly blurted out.

"They what?" the Professor asked incredulously, looking visibly shaken.

"But she said no. She wouldn't dignify it."

"The folks of Glendale County had it in for me from day one. Admit it."

Mary Anne grew thoughtful. "Not everybody. But Alex said I had to grow up and teaching you a lesson was part of it."

"What? That's crazy."

"Alex said that I have diminished mental capacity. Why? Why would he say such a thing?"

Professor West sat stoically in his chair, taking it all in. He said nothing.

"I'll tell you why," Mary Anne continued, answering her own question. "It's because he doesn't think that a man of your status could ever love me. And he's not alone in thinking that."

"Is that what this is all about? You and me?"

Mary Anne closed her eyes, afraid of the unknown. Maybe they were right all along. "I'm such a fool," she said, feeling embarrassed. "I've got to go," she said suddenly, and started to stand up but Professor West grabbed her arm. Reluctantly she sat back down again.

"Look at them!" Remington said, pointing.

"What a pig!" Critch said angrily.

"Mary Anne's smart enough to know better, isn't she?" Remington asked, sounding concerned.

"All I wanted to do was set you free. You're a butterfly and butterflies are free to fly…" Professor West said, his voice trailing off.

"What? Are you rejecting me?" Mary Anne exclaimed, horrified by the thought.

"Rejecting 'what' exactly?"

"The very idea of us. Does it repulse you? Is that what you're trying to tell me using metaphors to mask your aristocratic snobbishness?"

"Freedom is better than love," Professor West said, sounding eloquent, touching her with his words. "You have talent. Those bumbling idiots have no talent at all. Can't you see? They'll do anything to hold you back including making you doubt me…making you doubt yourself."

"Peter said I need a shrink."

"Peter's wrong," Professor West said. "Everyone's mental according to Peter. His whole world revolves around his psychiatrist like he's a satellite and she's a planet."

"In plain English please. I don't understand."

"I want you to be free of even me. That's how much I love you." Mary Anne slipped off her chair and passed out. Whether it was the alcohol speaking or whether she fainted, not even the bartender could say for sure.

Chapter 61

Mary Anne didn't know how she got home and into her own bed. She vaguely remembered Professor West on stage singing Karaoke—*Write! Write! Write it all out! These are the things that I'm talking about.* Was she dreaming or was she delusional? At what point did the lines between reality and fiction become blurred? Then it all fell into place like a completed puzzle. *Be mad or become a writer. Choose a side.* Professor West was now inside her head. *Harness your creativity and make a profit out of it!* What in God's green earth, pray do tell, happened last night?

Mary Anne looked in the mirror, lifted the toilet seat, held her hair back in a pony tail, and threw up. She didn't need a shrink to explain catharsis to her. She was destined for greatness and nobody except Professor West was willing to see it, not even herself. He was being persecuted for believing in her. And they had used her to plot against him. They'd rather call her delusional than for her to see her own potential as he did.

Mary Anne bit her lip and fought back tears but the flood gates opened anyway. She felt dirty and she felt cleansed and she fought against both and she embraced both. Oddly enough she felt exhilarated to be more neurotic than ever. Why? Because it was okay to not have it all figured out. She smiled without lipstick and pinched her lips, surprised that she was real after all. Mary Anne without the mask. Could she pull it off?

Chapter 62

Sandy Brosben was taking a batch of homemade oatmeal cookies out of the oven when the doorbell rang. She laid them on top of the stove, removed her oven mitts, and answered the door. It was a delivery man holding a bouquet of flowers. "Aren't you lucky," the delivery man said, beaming brightly as if he had personally sent them to her. "The third bouquet this week." She took the flowers and put them with the others in a large vase on the dining room table. She looked for a note but, like the others, there wasn't one. Tom, her husband, always sent a note with the flowers he had delivered to her. Sandy wondered who had taken a shine to her.

"You have to tell Tom," Jane Stanley said when she called her closest friend on the phone. "Otherwise he'll think you're having an affair."

"I know, I know, but how? Tom's on the road so much." Sandy's husband, Tom was a long-haul truck driver who was away most of the time.

"You'll find a way," Jane said comfortingly and hung up.

Sandy felt intimidated and frightened to be receiving flowers from an anonymous person. What if the sender of the flowers was a pervert, or a stalker? Maybe she should call the police. She started to dial 911 but lost her nerve and put the receiver down again. Then the phone rang. The voice on the other end said, "Did you get the flowers I sent? Aren't they lovely?" Then the caller hung up before Sandy could get in a word edge-wise.

"Definitely a stalker," Sandy said to herself. "First the flowers, now a phone call. And how did he know I had just received the flowers? Coincidence? She didn't think so. She lived in an apartment complex. Maybe she should move and change her phone number."

If it was a neighbor, who saw the florist van, and was pulling a prank on her, he would see Sandy throw the flowers out so that is what she decided to do. She marched outside, waving the bouquet of flowers over her head and shouted up at the windows, "Stop sending me flowers!" Then she marched back inside, locked the door, and poured herself a stiff drink. *My neighbors must think I've gone stark raving mad*, she thought. Then she laughed to herself. *How could she move without telling Tom, her husband? No, she decided, she would stay with her sister, Nancy Gilmoss who lived alone and had a spare bedroom.* Sandy had another shot of liquid courage and picked up the phone.

"Hi, baby sister," Nancy said. "Hey, what's wrong? You don't sound like your usual self."

"I've been getting flowers from a *Mr. Anonymous*. Three bouquets in one week. And today Mr. Anonymous called right after the flowers were delivered asking if I received them."

"I don't like the sounds of it. Why don't you stay here for a while till we get things sorted out?"

"I'd like that."

"Do you need a ride?"

"No, I'll take a cab."

"Mr. Anonymous might follow you here."

"He'd have to know I was going to take a cab and be waiting in his car in the parking lot in order to follow me. I think that's highly unlikely."

"Alright, I'll see you soon," Nancy said. "I'll put a pot of coffee on. Bring some of your home-baked cookies too."

Sandy checked to see if she had turned off the oven and cleaned up the kitchen. By now, her cookies had cooled down. She put them in a Tupperware container and packed them in a suitcase along with enough clothes to last a week. Then she called Holiday Taxi and waited in the lobby for her cab to show up.

When it did, Sandy got in and gave the driver her sister's address. She leaned back, exhausted. Then she took a couple of Valium pills out of her purse, popped them into her mouth and washed them down with Pepsi.

"You can't drink that in here," Herb, the driver, said.

"Oh, I'm sorry." She passed the can to Herb.

"Can't you see I'm driving?" Herb snapped. "You might as well finish it but don't leave any trash in the car when you get out."

"Gee, aren't you friendly," Sandy said sarcastically.

"What's that?"

"Cupid's stupid," Sandy mumbled as the Valium kicked in and she slid down in her seat, spilling the contents of the soda pop all over herself and the cab.

Chapter 63

Nancy was standing on the curb when the cab pulled up and she helped Sandy carry her luggage into the apartment. "Why don't you take a hot shower? You look a mess. There's a bathrobe on the hook behind the door."

"You're always thinking ahead," Sandy said appreciatively.

Nancy smiled. "What are sisters for?"

After her shower, Sandy came and sat down at the kitchen table and the two sisters talked about their lives over coffee and cookies. "I should call Tom and let him know I'm staying here for a while," Sandy finally said.

"Go ahead. You can use the kitchen phone or the one in the study."

Sandy tracked Tom down through the company dispatcher who said he was staying at the Ridgeway Motel. He answered on the first ring. She got right to the point. "Honey, somebody's been sending me flowers." There was silence on the other end of the line. Sandy didn't know how to interpret it.

"I've been sending you flowers. Didn't you get the cards that came with them?"

"No. None of the flowers I got had a card attached to them and somebody called up right after the last flowers were delivered to ask if I got them."

"I always send you flowers with a note," Tom said emphatically. "Did you recognize the voice on the phone?"

"No, but whoever it was could have disguised his voice."

"Why don't you ask Detective Joe Willis to check out the delivery man from the florist shop to see if he has a criminal record?"

"Honey, is that absolutely necessary?"

"I just want to make sure you're safe. Where are you now?"

"At Nancy's."

"Good. Stay there until I get back. It shouldn't be more than 2 or 3 days."

Sandy felt better knowing that the flowers were from Tom, but didn't know why someone would remove the notes. Three times. It could not be a coincidence. Why would somebody do this to her? She thought of possible enemies she might have but came up blank. She was a prisoner of fear.

An easy solution would be for her husband to buy her flowers when he got into town and hand deliver them. "Eureka!" she said aloud and Nancy gave her sister a puzzled look. "God works in mysterious ways," Sandy Brosben said simply as her face lit up.

"If you say so," Nancy said with a shrug. "I'm going to bed. Don't stay up too late."

The next morning Nancy got ready for work. She found her sister in the kitchen poking around in the fridge. "You'll have to fend for yourself," she told Sandy on her way out the door.

Sandy took a hot, leisurely bath. When she was finished soaking, she wrapped herself in a bath towel that her sister had laid out for her. Then she picked up the phone and called Tom who was waiting to hear from dispatch. "I've come up with a solution," she said optimistically.

"What is it?"

"Don't send me flowers. Bring them in person."

"Why didn't I think of that?" Tom asked.

"I'm more than just a pretty face," Sandy said. Tom and Sandy both laughed.

"Have a nice visit. I'll call you when I'm coming home. Sandy?"

"Yes?"

"I love you."

"I love you back." If only every problem could be this easy to fix, Sandy thought after hanging up. She looked in the fridge—onions, tomatoes, celery. She looked in the cupboards—spaghetti sauce, canned tomatoes, spaghetti noodles. "That's it. I'll whip up a mean dish of spaghetti," Sandy said to Felix, Nancy's spaded Egyptian Mau. Felix meowed, as if he understood, and she rewarded him by putting down a dish of Meow Mix and a bowl of fresh cream.

Chapter 64

The Dollhouse ladies met on Saturday night. Sandy Brosben was in attendance. She told them about the flowers and how she'd decided to deal with it. Bella Porter took a sip of her margarita and set it down gracefully, careful not to chip her perfectly manicured nails. "It seems to me that Sandy here has solved the problem without solving the mystery."

"What's wrong with that?" Maybelline asked.

"Yeah, what's wrong with that?" Jane Stanley echoed, standing by her childhood friend.

"Maybe nothing," Bella said. "But wouldn't you like to find out 'who' and 'why' to put your mind at ease?"

"Some things are better left alone," Marjorie said sagely, playing with one of her curls and finding a curler. Embarrassed, she quickly removed it and put it in her purse.

Bella raised an eyebrow. "Let's replenish our drinks," she suggested, opening the patio door and heading for the kitchen. The Dollhouse ladies faithfully followed.

"What florist do you get your flowers from?"

"Stephanie's Floral Arrangements on Victoria street. Why?"

"Because we could have flowers sent to each other with a card," Bella said excitedly.

"What would that accomplish?" Sandy asked.

"Pray do tell," Jane Stanley added, her curiosity equally piqued.

The Dollhouse ladies, drinks in hand, returned to their seats out on the patio. Bella removed the umbrella from her drink and took a thoughtful sip before speaking, "What it would accomplish would be to see if the notes will be removed or not."

"I don't follow," Marjorie said, wrapping her shawl around her tiny shoulders.

"If only the card for Sandy's flowers is missing, then we know that somebody is targeting Sandy Brosben specifically and nobody else," Bella said matter-of-factly.

"Even so, it still doesn't tell us who that somebody is," Jane commented.

"True," Bella continued, "but it gives us a place to start. Let's vote on it." The Dollhouse ladies began raising their hands, one by one. The only one who didn't raise her hand was Sandy.

"You're outnumbered," Bella whispered in Sandy's ear. They put their names into a hat and picked the name of the person they'd send flowers to. The note to Sandy would have to say 'from Tom'.

"Don't you think the flower shop will find it strange to have a bunch of ladies sending each other flowers?" Sandy asked.

"That's missing the point, my Dear. They'll appreciate the business," Bella said. "Monday morning, order your flowers with a card and have them delivered. We'll catch up next Saturday night with our findings." Bella slurped the last of her drink. The Dollhouse ladies did the same. They laughed in unison.

"Give us courage to change the things we can and the wisdom to know the difference, or something like that," Sandy Brosben mumbled to herself as she fell over and struggled to disentangle herself from her patio chair. Maybelline helped her up. "I can't believe we're doing this," Sandy confessed, as the ladies began dispersing.

"Believe it or not," Jane Stanley said, impersonating Ripley from Ripley's 'Believe it or Not'.

"Curiosity killed the cat," Bella said, looking at Maybelline.

Maybelline's face dropped, but she quickly regained her composure. "But satisfaction brought it back."

"You ladies have way too much time on your hands," Marjorie yelled over her shoulder as she walked toward Mary Anne's Chevy. Mary Anne helped her mother into the truck using the trusty footstool and walked around to the driver's side and got in. She honked the horn. The Dollhouse ladies honked back.

"See, this is what I love about Glendale," Mary Anne commented, squeezing her mother's hand. "We're all nuts but nobody cares."

"Speak for yourself," Marjorie snapped, removing the curler from her purse and finding a lock of hair to recurl. "Come on. Take me home."

Chapter 65

After the Dollhouse ladies had gone home, Bella Porter called Jane Stanley on the phone. "What I didn't want to say in front of Sandy is that if everyone gets a sweet nothing note with their bouquet of flowers, it puts Tom on top of the suspect list."

Jane's ears pricked up. "You think Tom could be sending Jane flowers without a note on purpose?"

"You didn't hear it from me, Jane."

"Why would he do that?"

"You know Sandy's a bit 'fragile' if the truth be known. Maybe Tom wants to 'tip her over the edge'."

"There are other ways. No, I don't think Tom's like that. Sandy knew Tom was a long-haul trucker when she met him. She's used to him being away for long stretches. There has to be a better explanation than that."

"We'll see," Bella said, sounding doubtful.

"Look here, Bella," Jane said. "Don't you go upsetting Sandy or you'll end up in the Doghouse."

"Oh, I'm sure that Al Critch won't mind that one bit," the conniving widow said as she hung up without saying goodbye.

Next Saturday came sooner than expected. The Dollhouse Ladies assembled in a circle on the patio like a reunion of Salem witches and soon drinks were flowing. They toasted each other, then Bella spoke. "Well ladies, what have you got?" After comparing notes, it was discovered that Sandy did get a card accompanying her flowers which read, *To Sandy, Love Tom.* "That rules out the delivery driver, honey," Bella said, reaching over to hold Sandy's hand comfortingly, but Sandy shook her hand free.

"I need another drink," Sandy said, getting up and sliding open the patio door. She made a beeline for the kitchen. Jane Stanley got up and followed her.

"There could be a hundred and one explanations," Jane said, pouring them each a drink from the blender.

"Yeah, and none of them good," Sandy said dismally.

"Look, you know the flowers you've been getting are from your husband, Tom, and he says he sends a note with them. That's what you have to hang onto," Jane said reassuringly. "Trust. Faith. Love. Mysteries are the devil's way to fuck with your head. Leave it alone. Pick a side."

"It was so much easier when I was a little girl in love with the boy next door."

"Tom?"

"Yeah, Tom."

"How so?" Jane asked, taking a sip of her drink and leaning up against the kitchen counter.

"Because back then," Sandy said, turning to face Jane, "I could pick the petals off my bouquet of daisies—*He loves me, he loves me not...*"

Jane's expression turned very serious, then suddenly the two women burst out laughing uncontrollably. "You'll be alright," Jane said, steering Sandy toward the patio. "What are friends for?"

Chapter 66

"Who's there?" Al Critch barked, opening the peep hole to the Doghouse.

"Mr. Periwinkle," Mr. Periwinkle said with a wink, hoisting up a 12-pack of beer for Al to see.

"Come in! Come in! I might as well invite the whole neighborhood," Al said in mock annoyance as Erno Federno and Alex Remington crowded into the Doghouse behind Reverend Periwinkle.

"What's up?" Erno asked, popping open a beer. It was Bring Your Own Beer night. Come to think of it, it was always BYOB night at the Doghouse.

"I thought you weren't allowed to drink after your heart attack," Critch said, looking worried.

"What Marjorie doesn't know can't hurt her. Besides, the Dollhouse Ladies don't do anything that we don't do."

"Oh, is that a fact?" Alex said, passing each man a big, fat joint.

"Spark it up, Sparky," Reverend Periwinkle said as they passed around Critch's lighter.

"You really are a Sunday morning preacher," Critch said reverently, inhaling deeply.

"Folks need a tune up every once in a while," the Reverend said with a twinkle in his eye. "Make them feel guilty and dirty. Make them feel innocent and clean. Then make them feel forgiven for unconfessed, unforgiveable sins. Allow them to embrace this, their humanness, so they do not feel isolated but freed. All I do is unlock that spiritual door for them and let the holy spirit do the rest."

"Sweet Jesus," Alex Remington said, feeling like the reincarnation of Doubting Thomas.

"Hey," Erno piped up. He was beginning to get stoned. "Alex, what's with the beads?"

"Oh, those. Myrtle put them in."

"The big black broad from the Five and Dime in Bullhead Narrows?" Erno asked. The men laughed and took a swig of their beer.

"It's not like that," Alex said. "We're just friends."

"Myrtle's got a thing for you," Erno said, grinning foolishly.

"No, she doesn't," Alex said defensively.

"Must be a shortage of black men in Bullhead Narrows because she sure tried to turn you into one," Critch said, and the men snickered. Alex shook his head and went outside to take a whiz.

"I doubt he's built like a horse though," Critch said in a low voice.

"I heard that," Remington snapped, returning to the Doghouse and grabbing a second beer from the fridge.

"Do you like her or not?"

"She's not my type," Alex said matter-of-factly.

"And April is?" Erno asked, leaning back, working on his second brewski.

"How do you know about April?" Alex asked, turning red. Erno ignored the question and concentrated on pulling the label off his beer without tearing it.

"You're a rescuer, Alex," Critch said. "You think April needs rescuing and that she could do better than Keystone. No offense about your brother, Erno, but Keystone will never leave Laura for a two-bit whore," Al Critch blurted out. Suddenly the Doghouse fell silent.

"Stand up, you piece of shit," Remington said, grabbing Critch by the shirt and hoisting him to his feet.

"Easy does it," Erno cautioned, standing up. He popped a couple of nitroglycerin tablets before turning to Critch. "That was uncalled for. Let sleeping dogs lie." Alex Remington slowly sat down again and so did Critch and Erno.

"What we all need is another joint," Reverend Periwinkle said.

"Amen to that," Erno exclaimed, and Alex Remington reached into his front pocket and took out four more joints.

"See," the Reverend said, "God does work in mysterious ways."

"So what are you going to do now, shit or get off the pot?" Erno asked.

"Shit," Remington said, inhaling deeply, and they all started laughing. They laughed so hard and so long that in their stoned minds they forgot what they were laughing for which made them laugh even harder.

"What does April think about your hairdo?" Erno asked at long last.

"I don't care what April thinks. That's what I love about her."

"For Heaven's sake, cut it all off," Erno said, looking both thoughtful and stoned.

"He should at least give Myrtle back her beads so she can find another guinea pig to practice on," Reverend Periwinkle suggested, then paused. "Did I just say that?"

"Okay, guys. You've had your fun," Alex said.

"Who's brave enough to cut them off?" Erno asked.

"Oh no you don't. I'm going to see Myrtle and have her cut my hair really short. Women love a clean-cut man."

"Some women," Erno reminded Alex, touching his ponytail to make sure it was still there.

"You can be a hippie without looking like one," Reverend Periwinkle pointed out, sounding wise. "I mean, as a pastime, but not front and center. Now that's unforgiveable."

"Yeah, I suppose I did overdo it."

"Well, prodigal son," the Reverend said, patting Remington on the shoulder. "I'm sure glad you've come to your senses, even though it took a little bit of pot and your buddies to bring you round." Critch opened the door to the Doghouse. The moon was full and their faces glowed in the moonlight. The fresh air felt good as the men stepped out of the man cave.

Chapter 67

"I guess we'd better be getting home," Erno said, "or our wives will start to worry about what we're up to."

"Wasn't life easier when we were boys and had our treehouse?" Alex asked.

"Until it was blown down," Critch replied.

"Our treehouse wasn't blown down. That's just what we were told," Erno interjected. "My old man thought it was going to fall down with all of us piled into it so he tore it down."

"Boy, you have the memory of an elephant, Erno."

"Yeah, well now it feels better to forget."

"With pot you live in the moment. It's your happy place and no one can steal it from you. It's yours," Alex said.

"Spoken like a true drug dealer," Critch commented, laughing at his own wit. He gave Reverend Periwinkle a wink, and the Reverend, eyes glazed over, started to fall backward but Critch caught him by the collar and he caught his balance again.

"What are you becoming, Pentecostal?" Critch teased.

"Remind me to put that in my sermon," Reverend Periwinkle replied, brushing himself off.

"Put this in your sermon," Alex Remington said, stuffing a big fat reefer into the Reverend's front pocket. "Better hide that from the missus though."

"There are worse things than inhaling," Reverend Periwinkle said, rationalizing his token of appreciation.

"Like?"

"Some things are best left unsaid."

"Was that a confession, Preacher?" Erno asked.

Periwinkle started to wink, but changed his mind. He squinted instead as if peering into Erno's soul.

"Deep. Very deep." He had no idea what he was talking about because one part of his mind was chasing the other and trying to catch up. That's what he liked about pot. The friggin' insight it gave him like God reaching into his mind and opening it up for him.

"Holy crap," Erno said. "You're reading my mind."

"Careful not to step in dog shit," Critch said, changing the subject as the men staggered down the center line that weaved through the Silver Fox Trailer park. "There're a few strays around. Dog catcher can't seem to catch them. I put a bowl out every night. In the morning, the dog food's gone."

"How do you know you're not feeding a stray cat?" the Reverend asked. "Or a raccoon?"

Al was taken aback like it was a slap in the face. "I know the difference between Goddamn dog shit and cat shit or whatever shit. Do you need me to explain it to you?"

"Some things are better left unsaid," Reverend Periwinkle repeated, rolling his eyes.

"I think I'll head back now," Critch said, looking up at the stars and the milky way. He turned back toward his trailer. Nobody ever stepped foot inside Al Critch's trailer. That was his sanctuary and he kept his sanctuary and the Doghouse separate. It was like he had a foot in both worlds and he'd given up a long ago trying to choose between the two.

The radio was still on inside the Doghouse and Hank Snow's 'Miller's Cave' lured him back inside his comfort zone. He opened the creaky door and shut it behind him. Then he sat down on the cot, took off his shoes, and laid back, pulling the woolen blankets over him. It was like sleeping outdoors in the fresh air. In no time, he was fast asleep, with the starry heavens smiling down on him.

Chapter 68

Professor West's office was in the basement of Glendale Community college. A bar fridge, microwave, and coffee maker gave the office a lived-in look, not to mention a beige, plaid davenport that opened into a bed for the nights when the Professor was too tired or too drunk to drive home. Having an office filled with books and his students' term papers made Professor West feel validated and legitimized. He took off his corduroy blazer and draped it over the back of his chair. Then he grabbed a towel and his gym keys and headed for the shower.

Jerry Thornapple, the janitor, was mopping the floors. "Why don't you sign up for one of my creative writing classes?" Professor West teased, half-serious.

"One of these days," Thornapple replied, wringing out his mop. Jerry Thornapple was in his early thirties. He wore his sandy, shoulder-length hair in a ponytail under a black bandana. He played lead guitar in a band called The Rubber Banditos on Saturday nights at various venues around Glendale, Bullhead Narrows, and Cedar Falls. "Marking papers kind of late, aren't you?" Jerry asked, leaning on his mop.

"Done for the night."

"Hey Professor," the security guard called out as Professor West rounded the corner, "I could set my watch to you."

The Professor smiled, "Say Tommy, did you ever find out who spray painted the lockers?"

"No, but I filled out a police report. Still waiting to hear back." Tommy Pickett used to get teased a lot in school by the town bullies who called him Tommy Pick Pocket because of his sleight of hand. Tommy sometimes moonlighted as a magician at children's birthday parties. Professor West continued down the hallway toward the showers. This was his favorite part of the day. He grabbed a towel and Head and Shoulders from his locker, stripped down to his bare buff, and stepped into the shower. The hot water soothed his aching muscles.

After 15 minutes, the Professor turned off the faucet and toweled dry. His mind drifted toward thoughts of Mary Anne. *It's easy to teach a student,* Professor West thought as he put on his pajamas, *but it's not easy to turn a student into a successful writer.* Yet he knew that his job was not to live his students' lives for them. He was just their springboard. *So if Mary Anne flops, he thought, at least she has the guts to try thanks to me. Maybe all Mary Anne is ever destined to be is ordinary and I can't accept that. Perhaps I pity her for trying harder than the others just to end up in the same place—Glendale. Nobody wants to leave the familiar behind and set out on their own when failure feels like loyalty and success feels like betrayal.*

Who's the neurotic one now? Professor West asked himself as he opened the locker room door and looked both ways. He looked a sorry sight in his pajamas, tattered towel, and flip flops. *What would my students think if they could only see me now?* He quickly made a beeline for his office and, once inside, locked the door. He made up his couch with fresh linens, then retrieved a flask of whiskey from a bottom drawer and took a swig. Exhausted, he laid down and pulled the blankets up around himself.

Glendale was his home even though his father had moved away so many years ago when he was just a snot-nosed kid in elementary school. He didn't even know his own mother. That was a hard pill to swallow. His own mother, his flesh and blood, had abandoned him. No mother would do that unless there was something wrong with him. He reached for the hand mirror on his desk and stared at the man in the mirror. What he was looking for he didn't know but whatever it was, it could not be found in the face of the man staring back at him. "For Christ's sake!" he said out loud, louder than he expected.

"Is everything alright in there?" Tommy Pickett asked, tapping on his door.

"I just forgot to call Mother but it's too late now," Professor West replied.

"Well, good night," Tommy said and Professor West could hear the security guard's footsteps retreating.

Chapter 69

Out of the piercing stillness, the telephone rang. "Suicide hotline," Professor West said when he picked up the receiver, knowing that it was probably Peter Carmichael.

"Very funny," Peter said.

"Do you have any idea what time it is?"

Peter ignored the question. "I finally figured out why Mary Anne has such a crush on you," Peter said enthusiastically.

"This had better be good," Professor West said.

"As long as Mary Anne is infatuated with you, she doesn't have to face her *neurotic* struggle."

"*Neurotic* struggle?"

"Between her fear of failure and her fear of success."

"I've never heard of anything so ridiculous. Couldn't this have waited?"

Undeterred, Peter continued, "You've got to encourage Mary Anne to start writing for herself and not for your approval."

"For herself?"

"That's what I just said."

"And you called me at 3:00 o'clock in the God damn morning just to tell me that?"

"You wouldn't be sleeping in your office if you had it all figured out," Peter said and hung up.

"Arrogant bastard!" the Professor yelled into the receiver. "Thanks for the free psychiatric advice!" Professor West decided to get some fresh air to clear his head. He refilled his flask of whiskey and hid it in his inside breast pocket. Then he walked down the corridor and opened the door to outside.

"Mary Anne without the Professor sounds a lot like a remake of Gilligan's Island," he could imagine Peter saying. He stared up at the poplar trees, listening to their leaves rustling in the breeze, searching for guidance. *Was God mocking him?*

Chapter 70

Professor West took a swig of whiskey and decided to go home. He returned to his office to pick up his briefcase and lock up. As he drove, he fantasized about Mary Anne becoming a masterful writer, not because she loved him anymore, but because she felt numb, and the only way she could express herself after being so hurt and rejected was through her fictional characters.

"God evened the score," he envisioned Mary Anne telling her mother at her book signing and telling him 'to take his holy grail and shove it where the sun don't shine'.

Suddenly Professor West was jarred out of his drunken reverie by a horn blaring directly behind him. "Hey old man, I don't have all day!" the driver behind him shouted. How he got from his davenport to his car he could not recollect. He must have blacked out.

Professor West rolled down his window and stuck his head out. "You can kiss my lily-white ass!" he shouted at the driver behind him and gave him the finger. Then he stepped on the gas.

"You son of a bitch!" the driver in his rear-view mirror shouted back and stepped on the gas too. This alerted the attention of a local cop who put on his siren in hot pursuit. Professor West nonchalantly turned the corner and parked in an alley as the car behind him got pulled over. He got out of his car, pulled down his zipper, and peed on his tires. Then he zig-zagged home. It took Professor West three attempts to park his car in the assigned stall behind his apartment at Valley View Drive. "The alignment's off," he explained to the paperboy who was standing on the sidewalk watching him.

"My dad's a mechanic," the paperboy volunteered.

"And mine's a rocket scientist," Professor West said with a smug smirk on his face, enjoying a good lie.

The paperboy grinned back. "Just ask Bugsy at Bugsy's Garage across town that you want a 10% discount. I'm Bugsy Junior. I get a commission for sending my old man work."

"I'll look into it," Professor West said, grabbing a newspaper.

"Hey, that's Thomas's paper."

"Thomas who works at the casino?"

"The very one."

"He's my neighbor. I'll bring it up to him on my way inside. Here. Take one of my business cards. Bugsy Junior took the card with a puzzled look on his face. Then he shrugged and stuffed the card into his pocket and carried on his newspaper route."

For a fleeting moment, Professor West wished that he could trade places with the simple paperboy with a simple plan. The professor looked up at the sky as night gave way to daybreak and saw a pair of Canadian geese making their way to their nesting grounds on the edge of Glendale County. They were honking back and forth.

"How did I become so very fucking uncivilized?" Horatio asked the heavens. In response, they opened up wide and something white and sticky landed across his cheek.

Chapter 71

Mary Anne rose early to get ready for work at Dino's Diner. It was Friday, the busiest day of the week. She reached for some bread to make some toast, and then decided she'd get a fast bite at work. *Saves on the grocery bill*, she thought, grabbing her cardigan and scooting out the door.

"Hi Mary Anne," Wendy said when Mary Anne came through the door. "Looks like you didn't get much sleep last night." Mary Anne yawned agreeably as she hastily put on her apron and took out a writing pad from under the cash register.

"Maybelline's teaching Belinda Jane how to make apple pie. She's become quite the entrepreneur," Wendy said, making small talk. Mary Anne smiled and then her mouth dropped as in walked none other than the notorious Professor West. He looked around the tiny dining room and decided to take a coffee to go.

"How do you take it?" Mary Anne asked, trying not to blush.

"Straight up just the way I like—" Professor West cut himself off mid-sentence and recovered quickly—"my eggs." He did not want to appear vulgar. Mary Anne gave him a puzzled look. "Sunny side," the Professor explained.

"Do you want to see the breakfast menu?"

"No, I'm running late."

"How about a slice of Maybelline's notorious apple pie?"

"No, it'll go straight to my waist."

"You could use a few pounds," Mary Anne said. "You're too skinny."

"What the Professor needs is a good woman to fatten him up. One that's handy in the kitchen," Wendy said, grinning shamelessly.

"Wendy!" Mary Anne scolded, poking the younger waitress in the ribs. "Professor West said he's running late." Mary Anne held out the Professor's coffee like it was the holy grail. He took his coffee, lifted his hat, and bowed courteously, and then left as quickly as he had come.

"He's trying to impress you."

"Yeah, but he stinks of alcohol," Mary Anne commented as she made her way over to the counter to serve the construction workers. They were lined up for their usual Big Breakfasts with ham, bacon, and sausage, and, of course, Dino's coveted homemade hash browns.

"He doesn't know what he's missing," George, the foreman, said.

"What?" Mary Anne asked, her mind still reeling.

"I was referring to the Big Breakfast."

"Oh," Mary Anne replied, noticeably deflated.

"What did you think I meant?"

"More coffee?" Wendy asked, coming to Mary Anne's rescue.

"There's a table over by the window that needs cleaning," Dino said to Mary Anne as he came barreling out of the kitchen. Dino asked the construction workers how they liked the hash browns and made a point of telling them that they were homemade. Then he poured himself a cup of black coffee before returning to the kitchen.

"It's either Dino's mellowing or we're getting used to him," Mary Anne said, laughing. Wendy laughed too.

"Get back to work. I don't pay you to stand around and make joke," Dino bellowed, banging the pots and pans. Mary Anne busied herself picking up empty plates and Wendy went around with the coffee pot, pouring refills into empty cups, not bothering to ask whether the customers wanted a refill or not.

Chapter 72

"Refill to go?" Mary Anne asked Nancy as she rang up Nancy's bill.

"Not today. I see *your* Professor was in this morning. Isn't Dino's out of the way," Nancy commented.

"*My* Professor? Since when did Professor West become *my* Professor?" Mary Anne asked, playing dumb.

Nancy ignored the question. "He's totally into you."

"That's not what I hear. Besides, we have nothing in common."

"You like writing, don't you?"

"Nothing that anyone would care to read."

"I wouldn't be so sure. You do keep a diary, don't you?"

"How do you know about my diary?"

"Lucky guess," Nancy replied, and winked. She could see where this was going and wisely made her exit. The rest of the day was uneventful except for Jerry Thornapple and the Rubber Banditos who came into Dino's at lunch time to order steak and eggs.

"Breakfast was over an hour ago," Mary Anne said, "and Dino won't bend the rules for nobody."

"Okay, we'll take some homemade pan fries if they're still available, otherwise fries with gravy on the side."

"Say, where are you guys playing this weekend?"

"The Sundance Saloon. Last time we played there some dude got himself hog-tied in the back alley. I doubt he'll be showing his face around there for some time," Jerry said, laughing.

"Oh, that was Keystone's doing. He's my uncle. Sort of," Mary Anne replied, carting off some dirty dishes from a nearby table. "Maybe Maybelline and I will come hear you play."

"Yeah, that'd be cool. We're expecting a big crowd because it's Troy Pickett and Lisa Conway's pre-wedding party."

"Troy's Tommy Pickett's son. He used to play back up guitar for us before he got a job with Lisa's father at the hardware store. You know Lisa Conway, don't you?"

"Isn't she from Cedar Falls?"

"I think so. Anyway, Troy's inviting the whole senior football team."

"That I gotta see," Mary Anne said over her shoulder as she scurried over to the next table. "The usual, Mrs. Periwinkle?" Mary Anne asked politely.

"Soup de jour with grilled cheese as usual," Mrs. Periwinkle said.

"I'll have the same," Reverend Periwinkle piped up, coughing a bit and smelling like marijuana. Mrs. Periwinkle shot him a hard look, if looks could kill. When Mary Anne disappeared to put their order in to the kitchen, she could hear Mrs. Periwinkle scolding her husband, who looked truly penitent.

Dino let Mary Anne off early so she could take Marjorie to a doctor's appointment. She threw down her apron and headed out the door, not a care in the world. *Why did people want her to be something more than happy?* Mary Anne thought as the Chevy hit every pothole on the way back to the Silver Fox trailer park.

Chapter 73

It was 4:00 o'clock in the morning and dark outside. Erno rolled out of bed and stretched. Marjorie was still asleep. How she could sleep with those big pink curlers in her hair, he didn't know. Erno showered, shaved, and put on his track suit and joggers. "Git 'er done!" he said to his reflection in the mirror while adjusting his headband. Then he headed over to Al's and banged on the Doghouse door.

Al wasn't expecting Erno but that didn't matter. Al was used to being on call and always willing to help out a friend, especially for a case of beer or a bag of weed. But he wasn't prepared for what was on the other side of the big, wooden door when he opened it.

"This had better be a real emergency," Al said, reaching for his coveralls and hammer.

"You won't need those today, my friend." Erno reached into his backpack and pulled out a pair of jogging shoes and a track suit with a big 'M' on the sleeve.

"Here, put these on," Erno prompted.

"You've got to be kidding."

"Do I look like I'm kidding?" Erno asked, jogging on the spot.

"What's wrong? If you have to use the bathroom, you can go behind that tree over there!" Al said, pointing with his chin.

"Just warming up. Come on. Get dressed. You're going to be my jogging partner today."

"Jesus, just give me five minutes, would you? I have to get the sawdust out of my ears," Al said, reaching for a face cloth and a bar of soap. He filled a basin full of water from a jug sitting in the corner. Then Al shoved a pair of clippers in Erno's direction. "Here, make yourself useful. You can cut the weeds along the driveway while I wash up and get dressed." Without waiting for a reply, Al shut the Doghouse door in Erno's face.

Chapter 74

Five minutes later, Erno and Al could be seen jogging side by side down the middle of the road. "Let's circle the trailer park and then head into town," Erno said to Al, hardly missing a beat. "Then we can stop at Dino's for a light breakfast."

"Sounds good to me," Al said, already starting to sweat. "When did you start jogging?"

"Today. I've got a second lease on life so I'd better show *The Man Upstairs* some gratitude."

"Stop!" Al shouted, feeling winded. "Let me catch my breath."

"Okay, you can powerwalk and I'll jog alongside you."

"Say what?"

"Powerwalk. It's walking fast and swinging your arms to go even faster."

"Who're you trying to lose weight for?" Al asked, trying to keep up. "Did you get a mistress?"

"You sound just like Marjorie," Erno replied, stopping to rest. He mopped his brow with a handkerchief and took a swig from his water bottle before passing it along to Al.

"Does Marjorie know?"

"She's asleep. I didn't want to wake her." They rounded the corner. Bella Porter had just gotten up and donned her housecoat. She put the kettle on the stove to boil and looked out her kitchen window. *Was she seeing things?* She grabbed her binoculars for a second look. *Was that Erno jogging? That was a first.* Bella picked up the phone and immediately called Marjorie.

"What?" Marjorie asked when Bella related the news. "Are you sure?"

"Yeah I'm sure. Al is wearing your track suit with the big letter 'M' on the sleeve."

"That big old snake!" Marjorie said, referring to Erno. "I bet he's found another woman and suddenly wants to get in shape."

"Don't jump to any conclusions," Bella said, sounding worried. "Why don't I come around with the car and we'll try to intercept them?"

"I'm all for it," Marjorie said. "Hurry!"

"You got it," Bella replied and promptly hung up. Marjorie rushed to the washroom and struggled to remove her curlers. Then she put on some clothes and her shawl and headed out onto the porch.

"Mother. What's going on? Have you lost your mind?" Mary Anne asked.

"Erno's out jogging with Al Critch who happens to be wearing my track suit!"

"Good God!" Mary Anne exclaimed, putting her hand over her mouth.

"Bella's coming over and we're going to track them down."

Chapter 75

"Go easy on him, Marjorie," Mary Anne cautioned. Mary Anne followed her mother out to the front porch where her mother was busy peeling off the paint with her chipped fingernails. "I don't know what else to do."

"You could always get Al Critch to repaint it," Mary Anne suggested.

"That's not what I mean. I don't know what to do about Erno. Look, there's Bella now," Marjorie said, sounding both frantic and hopeful as Bella pulled up, honking her horn. Mary Anne helped her mother down the steps and into the car.

"Don't forget this," Mary Anne said, passing Marjorie her weathered cane. She looked over at Bella. "Whatever you do, don't run them over." Then she went back inside, the screen door rattling in protest.

Chapter 76

The two arch enemies, except under extenuating circumstances, caught up with the odd couple hobbling and jogging toward downtown. Bella honked her horn but Erno waved them away dismissively and kept on jogging.

"Roll down your window," Bella ordered Marjorie and Marjorie complied.

"Erno!" Marjorie cried out, poking her cane out the window and trying to poke Erno with it.

"Put that damn thing away before someone gets hurt!" Erno shouted.

"What on earth are you doing?"

"I'm trying to get fit."

"Why? Aren't your pills working?"

Erno stopped jogging and Bella pulled over and put the car in park. "I want to be around to take care of you," Erno said. Marjorie didn't know how to respond to that but was secretly touched.

"Where are you headed?"

"Dino's Diner."

Bella had an idea. "We'll meet you there and drive you two home afterward. That'll be enough of a workout for one day." Reluctantly, Erno grunted and nodded at the same time.

At Dino's Diner, Dino personally came to their table and distributed menus. "Mary Anne's told me a lot about you," Marjorie said, sliding into her seat and hooking her cane on the edge of the table. "This is Erno, my husband. He's taken up jogging."

Patting his potbelly, Dino replied, "I should take up jogging too. Would you like the Early Bird breakfast?"

"What's that?" Erno asked, taking off his headband and wiping his forehead with a napkin.

"One egg, toast, hash browns, and your choice of bacon, ham, or sausage."

"Sure. I'll have it with bacon," Erno said, and the others decided to have bacon as well.

"Make sure my bacon is crispy," Marjorie said, "and I'll have tomato slices instead of hash browns."

Dino felt offended. "No substitutions."

"Oh," Marjorie replied, crestfallen.

"But you can have a side of tomatoes," Dino quickly added.

"Alright, but put my hash browns on Erno's plate, and not too many. He's had a heart attack," Marjorie explained.

Dino nodded solemnly and collected the menus hastily. Then he went back to the kitchen to prepare their breakfasts.

Chapter 77

"Look who just walked in," Bella exclaimed, staring at the Creative Writing Professor.

"I don't know what Mary Anne sees in him," Erno said critically. "Kind of scrawny, ain't he?"

"Must be love," Marjorie said dreamily. She smiled and nudged Erno. "Don't you remember what it felt like to fall in love for the very first time?"

"No. Jog my memory," Erno replied, and then started to laugh at his own play on words. That broke the ice and soon the whole table was laughing.

Professor West suddenly felt like he was under a microscope. Were they laughing at him? He looked down at his pants, afraid that he was still wearing his pajama bottoms but he had changed into his slacks. Even so, he concluded that they must be laughing at 'him'. That is when Horatio did an uncharacteristic thing. He took the bull by the horns and walked over to their table.

"What seems to be so funny?" the Professor asked hauling up a chair. He turned it backward and straddled it.

"Erno has taken up jogging," Bella replied, snickering behind a napkin while pretending to wipe her mouth.

"You should be encouraging him to improve himself. The fact that he's self-motivated is a plus," the Professor pointed out.

"Do you think so?" Marjorie asked, sounding like a little schoolgirl, unsure of herself.

"Of course. He's on a quest. Mess with that and you get left behind," the Professor added, grabbing a strip of bacon off Erno's plate. "Watch your cholesterol, Erno. You're going to want to be around to watch your grandchildren grow up."

Suddenly you could hear a pin drop and all eyes fastened on Professor West. "What grandchildren?" Marjorie asked, suspicion in her voice.

"Calm down the two of you," Al Critch cautioned, sensing a storm brewing. "It's just an expression."

"Oh. I get it," Bella said, like she'd figured out the missing piece of the puzzle.

"Whatever it is you think you've figured out, Bella," Professor West said, "I suggest you keep it under your hat," and he made an origami hat out of a paper placemat and plopped it on Bella's head for emphasis. *Look who's laughing now*, he thought as he headed out the door, the chimes ringing loudly as he made his departure.

"He's got a point," Al said, stuffing the last morsel of toast into his mouth, and washing it down with coffee. Al put his spare change on the table for a tip.

"You don't have to tip Dino," Marjorie said. "He owns the joint."

"Well, I'm not going to untip him. Leave the change alone."

"Who's going to pay? Any volunteers?" Bella Porter asked, removing her paper origami hat and unfolding it quizzically to see how it was made.

"Erno was the one who suggested Dino's," Al commented, "so logic dictates that he should pay for everybody."

"You're pretty cheap, aren't you Al?" Bella pointed out, giving up on her paper hat and pushing it aside.

"The way I see it," Al said, ignoring Bella's dig, "is that Erno should pay for my meal to compensate me for being his jogging partner."

"Alright, alright, you win," Erno said, sorting through some fives and tens to get to his twenties. He always kept a thick wad of bills in his wallet. Three hundred dollars of it he never spent, just to look like he had money whenever he opened his wallet in public.

"I don't know why you keep so much money in your wallet, Erno," Marjorie scolded. "You're just asking to be mugged."

"Leave him alone," Al said. "The man's got his pride."

Marjorie reached for her cane and stood up. "Bella, walk me to the car, would you, before I wrap this cane around Erno's neck." Bella did as she was told.

Erno walked up to the cash register. "I'll tell you what," Dino said, ringing in Erno's bill. "If you're going to start coming here regularly, I'll give you a 25% discount."

"Fair enough," Erno said, smiling at the idea of having someone in his corner.

"Us guys got to stick together," Dino said conspiratorially. He poured himself a cup of coffee, then added, "I've got to get back to my hash browns before they stick to the grill."

Chapter 78

That night, Erno tossed and turned. Sleeping with Marjorie and those curlers was like sleeping with a porcupine. "If you don't like it, you can sleep on the sofa," Marjorie scolded.

"Why don't you sleep on the sofa?" Erno shot back. Marjorie turned away from her long-suffering husband. The conversation was over.

"How did we get from foreplay to this?" Erno asked himself. He got up to look at his flabby belly and thighs in the full-length mirror. He certainly didn't want to look at his dimply buttocks. Mirrors never lie. It's a good thing they didn't talk. "Mirror, mirror on the wall. Who's the…Oh, never mind." Erno looked in the fridge. Then he closed it. He wondered what he'd look like if he was fit and trim and healthy? He was sixty-one years old. He'd taken an early retirement when he started having heart trouble. "Arrhythmia. Irregular heartbeat. You should take better care of yourself," his family doctor had said. Was it too late?

Erno returned to the bedroom and turned the night light on. He leaned over and studied Marjorie's face. In the shadowy light, it looked like she was sleeping with one eye open. He jumped back reflexively and squeezed his eyes shut to erase the image from his mind. Then he turned off the night light, grabbed his pillow and headed for the chesterfield. It was already made up with fresh sheets and a blanket. He didn't believe for a moment that it was because he snored. That was because he'd never heard himself snoring. "Trust me," Marjorie would say. "When you snore, the whole trailer shakes."

Chapter 79

That night, he slept with the living room curtains open. He would wake up with the daylight instead of an alarm. More natural. It was 7:00 AM when he awoke. The first thing he noticed was that he was stiff and sore all over. *How am I going to jog if I can hardly move?* he thought.

"You'll get used to it," Al Critch said cheerfully, helping himself to a second cup of coffee, "or die trying."

"Thanks for the pep talk," Erno replied, waddling butt naked across the room to retrieve his housecoat.

"Have you no sense of modesty?" Al scolded.

"Modesty? Ha! If you don't like the size of it, cover your eyes."

Chapter 80

Ten minutes later, the Mutt and Jeff duo were once again huffing and puffing around the trailer park. Bella Porter was retrieving the Glendale Herald from the mailbox at the end of her driveway wearing only her bathrobe and slippers when they jogged past. "How long are you two clowns going to keep this up?" Bella shouted.

"As long as we have a captive audience," Erno hollered back, jogging on the spot. Al Critch jogged on the spot too, a silly grin on his face.

"Why don't you join us?" Al asked.

"It would take me too long to put on my face. Maybe another time," Bella said dismissively as she headed back to her trailer. She had already started reading the newspaper before she went back inside.

"Probably reading the obituaries," Al said.

"How else is she going to know she's still alive?" Erno added jokingly.

Al pondered this a moment. "That was a joke, right?" Erno shook his head. Al was a lot of things but bright wasn't one of them.

"Al, I feel like jogging alone today. Do you mind?"

"Whatever you say. I'm supposed to mow the Periwinkles' lawn this morning anyway."

"By the way, Marjorie wants her track suit back. Says you should get yourself one with a big 'A' on the sleeve. What do you say, *Asshole?*"

"Now you know that's not very nice," Al said, feigning hurt feelings. Erno shrugged, and boxed the air mockingly before heading off in the opposite direction. As he jogged, his senses became invigorated. He heard the black-cheeked chickadees calling to each other and saw them flit among the pine branches. Cotton candy clouds floated lazily across the sky. Maybelline's sprinkler was on and one of her toms was trying to decide how to get to the front door without getting wet. Finally, he decided to go around.

Walkers and joggers and young mothers pushing strollers peppered the sidewalk leading into town. Erno was not the only one trying to get in shape. Yet it was obvious that his decision to get in shape made Marjorie feel more insecure than she already was. When she was drunk, the smallest thing would tick her off and she'd start throwing things at him, anything within reach. "You have to learn better communication skills," Erno would say and Marjorie's only answer was, "We need more dishes."

The light had turned red. Erno jogged on the spot, waiting for it to turn green again. Nancy Gilmoss honked and rolled down the window to shout hello. She gave him the thumbs up and smiled. Erno smiled back.

Chapter 81

When Erno arrived at the Diner, Mary Anne was pouring the construction crew refills of coffee and taking away their dirty dishes. Erno gave Mary Anne a kiss on the cheek before sitting down at the counter.

She was about to pour coffee for him but he put his hand over the cup. "I'll take decaf, along with a discount," Erno said matter-of-factly, then added, "because it's decaf."

"Yep, you're Keystone's brother alright, always watching the pocketbook. Say, could you put that wad of money you always carry around with you in your Will?"

"Got a pen?" Erno asked the construction worker sitting beside him.

"Will a carpenter's pencil do? Name's Pierre."

"Thanks. I'm Erno." Erno wrote on a napkin, 'The wad of money in my wallet I bequeath to Mary Anne.' "Will you be a witness, Pierre?" Pierre LaRose promptly signed his name as a witness. "I need two witnesses. How about the man sitting next to you?"

"Sure," Chris Logan pipped up and signed the napkin too. Erno folded the napkin and scrawled 'Living Will' on it and passed it to Mary Anne.

"Plant one right here," Erno said, pointing. Mary Anne gave her step-father a peck on the cheek. "I'm only half Italian so you can forget about the other cheek." The construction workers started laughing riotously.

"You're a funny guy," Pierre said admiringly.

"How very cheeky of you," Chris Logan chimed in.

Dino came out of the kitchen just then wiping his greasy hands on his equally greasy apron. Mary Anne wondered when he'd washed it last. Probably never. Dino poured himself a cup of coffee while Mary Anne presented Erno with the Early Bird Breakfast.

"What's this? It looks pretty skimpy compared to last time."

"I took 25% off so I gave you 25% less food," Dino said. "Business is business."

"I don't know who's cheaper, you or Al," Erno said.

"Who's Al?" Dino asked, sounding perplexed.

"The handyman."

"Oh 'that' Al," Dino said. "Yeah, I know him. He sometimes comes here to wash dishes and to bus tables when we're short-staffed, especially when there's a game over at Glendale High. We get flooded afterward."

Mary Anne passed Dino on the way to the dish pit carrying some dirty dishes. On her way back from loading the dishwasher, she told Dino about Erno's Will. "I have to put it in my purse before I forget and do something stupid like blow my nose on it," she said to Dino, displaying the napkin proudly.

"Is it dated and signed?" Dino asked, apparently an expert on such matters. Mary Anne shook her head, and sashayed out through the swinging doors again. She passed the sacred napkin back to Erno. "Dino said you have to date and sign it." Erno rolled his eyes and asked Pierre for his carpenter's pencil once again, dated and signed it, and waved the napkin over his head like it was the national flag.

"Here ye witness."

"Here we witness," Pierre and Chris repeated in unison.

"That's a pretty respectable napkin now," Mary Anne exclaimed, beaming from ear to ear. She kissed it, then went to the back office and squirreled the napkin safely away in her purse.

"Don't blow it," Dino warned. Mary Anne looked puzzled.

"Dino tell joke."

"Ah-huh," Mary Anne said, pointing a finger at her temple, flicking it upward and rolling her eyes at the same time.

"If that's the way you apply mascara, you're in trouble," Dino said as he started filling the sink with hot soapy water and dirty pots and pans. "Crazy girl," he mumbled to himself.

"I heard that," Mary Anne shouted and Dino started banging the pots and pans even louder.

"That's no way to show your boss respect," Erno said sternly, polishing off his orange slice and leaving the peel.

"That's supposed to be the garnish to make the plate look more attractive. You're not supposed to eat it," Mary Anne reminded him.

"You can leave *your* garnish when it's on *your* plate. I'll eat *my* garnish when it's on *my* plate, fair enough?"

"Fair enough," Mary Anne said, handing Erno the bill.

"You forgot my double discount—25% off from Dino and 25% off from *Your Royal Highness.* That's 50% off," Erno protested, after studying it closely.

"Did I hear my name being used in vain?" Dino asked.

"Just negotiating Erno's bill. He says he gets 50% off."

"Mary Anne, do you have to be such a moron?" Erno asked in hushed tones.

"Look Erno. Dino checks every bill that's rung in the cash register at the end of the night." Mary Anne leaned over conspiratorially and whispered in Erno's ear. "But I'll ring it in as a muffin. He won't know the difference."

That made Erno smile. "You just made my day, *Little Cookie Crumb.*"

"Bye Dino!" Erno shouted in the direction of the kitchen.

There was no reply. "Dino's deaf but only when he wants to be," Mary Anne said. She switched to a whisper, "That means he likes you."

"Oh," Erno mouthed, clueing in and smiling mischievously. He reached for the door handle, the wind chimes marking the invisible boundary between Dino's world and the world outside.

Chapter 82

A brown car of indeterminate make and model slowed to a crawl beside Erno. The front windows were rolled down. "Wanna lift on account of your recent heart surgery?" Detective Joe Willis asked.

"No thanks, Dickhead. I'm out for some exercise." Erno resumed jogging and Detective Joe Willis continued driving at a snail's pace. Erno and Joe went to the same school together up to the fifth grade and then Joe's parents divorced and he went to live with his aunt in Medicine Hat, Alberta.

"What's this? A personal escort?" Erno asked.

"Oh, just passing time," Joe said nonchalantly, but his piercing blue eyes said otherwise.

"What's wrong, got tired of herding buffalo?" Erno asked, half-serious, half-joking, not knowing which side of Joe to appeal to.

"I heard that a motley crew from the Silver Fox Trailer park fixed Alex Remington's trailer…in a hurry I might add."

"What's wrong with that? Ain't a man allowed to have friends?"

"Did you know he took out insurance on the trailer?" Detective Joe Willis said smugly, warming up.

"Did you know that he never put in a claim to collect on the insurance," Erno shot back just as smugly.

"Who'd you hear that from?"

"I don't know. Word gets around."

"Al Critch?"

"I said," Erno repeated through clenched teeth, "I *don't* know."

"Well, how'd he come up with enough money to get the trailer fixed so fast?" Detective Joe Willis asked with renewed persistence.

"He called in a few favors, that's all."

"Must be pretty popular, that Alex Remington," Detective Joe Willis said, lighting a cigarette and wrestling with the steering wheel.

"Friends work for friends for free if there's a case of beer waiting for them at the end of the day," Erno said. "You know, you really shouldn't smoke those cancer sticks," he added pompously, and turned into a side alley between the drug mart and liquor store. Detective Joe Willis turned the steering wheel sharply in hot pursuit and drove the front end of the car up onto the sidewalk. A flask of whiskey on the car seat beside him tumbled onto the floor. Joe didn't know what to do first, put the car in reverse or flounder around for his flask. He decided on the latter.

"Smile, you're on candid camera!" Honey said as she leaned against Detective Joe Willis' front door, flashing her cleavage. She adjusted her hot pink mini-skirt and smiled broadly for the reporter from the Glendale Herald.

Chapter 83

Marjorie chose the slot machine in the far corner of the Lucky Slots casino. She held her rabbit's foot tightly and blew on it for good luck, scrunching her eyes tightly shut. "Come on God! Come through for me!" Then she wiggled into her seat and pulled with all her might on the big brass arm. God's arm. If good God was in the luck, then she was a believer, that was for damned sure. As the machine's bells and whistles announced her play—a cherry, another cherry, a row of cherries—she opened her eyes wide. Suddenly the machine was coughing out change left, right, and center. Marjorie grabbed her handbag to catch her windfall. She looked a sight holding the bag between her knobby knees and balancing herself with her bum jutting out like a teeter totter which didn't know whether to teeter or totter.

"Holy smokes! Marjorie hit the jackpot!" Thomas announced to Mary Anne. "Look at her rock!"

"Oh my God, that rabbit's foot of hers really kicked butt this time," Mary Anne exclaimed, disembarking from her stool and downing her lady's drink. Was it half price drinks because it was ladies' night or because Thomas was bartending? She could never tell which one it was and didn't dare ask, deciding that it was better to feel special and interpret the facts as she saw fit. It was kind of like a role reversal. When she was at work at Dino's, yeah, she laid on the charm. It was part of her job to flirt but Dino would warn her in his thick European accent, "Don't date the customers or you're fired on your ass."

"Ask Marjorie to leave me a tip," Thomas called after Mary Anne as he shook his tip jar and winked. Mary Anne looked over her shoulder and threw Thomas a coquettish smile, swinging her handbag as she rushed over to her mother's rescue.

"Help get this God damn thing off me!" Marjorie hollered when she saw Mary Anne. Somehow in her excitement the strap of her handbag had become wrapped around the slot machine lever, likely in a frenzied attempt to tie down her windfall.

"Thomas wants a tip, Mother," Mary Anne teased as they shuffled over to the bar. "It's ladies' night. How about a celebratory drink?"

"Why the Hell not?" Marjorie shoved her purse toward her daughter. "Here, hang onto this for me while I hoist myself onto the bar stool. I don't know why they have to make them so high anyway."

"On the house!" Thomas said as Mary Anne took out five dollars in change from Marjorie's purse and put it in Thomas's tip jar. "What are you going to do with your windfall?" Thomas asked, passing Marjorie a Lady's Slipper with an umbrella in it.

Marjorie removed the umbrella superstitiously and laid it gently on a napkin. "Who knows? I'm still in shock."

Thomas nodded, and continued examining the bar glasses, holding each one up to the light to check for spots.

"I don't know why you bother doing that, Thomas? Nobody's going to see the spots when the glass is full anyway," Marjorie pointed out.

"Because it's my job to be conscientious."

"You could make a living at that. Come over to our trailer and I'll show you what I mean."

"Mother, are you criticizing how I wash dishes?" Mary Anne asked, gearing up for a mother-daughter cat fight.

"Hey ladies. Time out. I'm not paid enough to referee," Thomas teased light-heartedly, and started picking up the empties at the other end of the bar.

"Saucy, ain't he?" Marjorie said. "Hey, Thomas, I'll have another two."

Thomas made a Lady's Slipper and placed it respectfully in front of Marjorie. Marjorie looked at the drink disappointedly. "I said another t-w-o."

"Oh, t-w-o," Thomas said, playing dumb. "You're not driving, I hope."

"I haven't driven in years, Honey. The only thing I drive these days is everybody crazy." Marjorie reached for her cane and misjudged. Suddenly she started leaning sideways in free fall.

"Timber!" Mary Anne shouted and caught her mother in midair.

Chapter 84

Bartending 101. *The customer's always right, especially a drunk.* "Maybe you'd like to sit at a table where the seats are more comfortable," Thomas volunteered.

"Thank you," Mary Anne said, "And can you keep Marjorie's handbag behind the counter until we pay our tab? We won't accept charity." Thomas nodded solemnly and their drinks were promptly moved over to a deuce and the chairs were pulled out. Thomas helped Marjorie with her chair and asked where she'd like her cane.

"Just hang it on the railing, dear." Marjorie said, "It's got my initials on it so nobody gets any funny ideas."

"Who'd want to steal a cane?" Mary Anne asked.

"Who'd want to steal my track suit with the big letter 'M' on it?" Marjorie shot back.

"Erno means well," Mary Anne exclaimed helplessly. "He just doesn't always go about things the right way. You know, he put me in his Will?" Mary Anne blurted out, suddenly changing the subject.

"He what?" Marjorie asked, scrutinizing Mary Anne.

"Oh, just that wad of money that he carries around in his wallet. He bequeathed it to me."

"When was this? Why wasn't I informed?" Marjorie demanded, her sharp staccato voice carrying throughout the casino.

"Shush, Mother. Everybody can hear you." Marjorie polished off her Lady's Slipper and reached for the other one.

"If the slipper fits, wear it!" Marjorie said as she took a swig and splashed it down the front of her frilly, white blouse.

Mary Anne stifled a laugh. "Oh, Cinderella. Let me clean that up!" She dabbed at her mother's blouse.

"Stop that, people are beginning to stare."

"They've been staring all along, Mother. You just haven't noticed. Where's that sequined shawl you always carry around with you?"

"At the bottom of my purse."

"Here, put this on," Mary Anne said, "removing her cardigan and wrapping it around her mother's shoulders. It'll hide your blouse, at least until we get home." Mother and daughter polished off their drinks and stood, lady-like, by the counter waiting for Thomas to look their way. When he did, he reached under the counter and passed over Marjorie's handbag.

"There's a cashier beside the gift shop," Thomas said, pointing. "You can cash in your windfall for a cashier's cheque."

Marjorie patted Thomas's hand. "Thanks, Thomas. I dunno what we'd do without you," Marjorie said, beginning to slur her words. Mary Anne pulled out $15 dollars and laid the money on the counter to cover the tab. "Keep the change, Thomas."

Chapter 85

Alex Remington sat at the kitchen table of his patched-up trailer reading the Glendale Herald. He took a sip of coffee and worked on the crossword, as was his morning ritual. Then he sat back and sighed, reflecting on all the rumors he had heard through the grapevine about a so-called gun floating around. He smirked because he was the one who had started the rumor. And he smirked even more when the rumor eventually got back to him entangled with all the conspiracy theories like a fishing net with barnacles attached to it. *Oh, what tangled webs we weave, when we practice to deceive.*

The latest gossip from the Dollhouse ladies was that Remington had committed armed robbery and stashed his gun in Maybelline's trailer to cast blame on the Cat Lady who would then turn around and cast blame on Al Critch if need be. But the truth of the matter was that it was all an elaborate lie because Remington knew it was easier for the folks of Glendale County to believe a lie than the truth. They would never in a million years believe that Remington had beaten Keystone fair and square in a game of high stakes poker. And why not? Because they were convinced that Keystone was light years ahead of Remington.

That being said, the sordid rumor was a game of revenge on the simple folks of Glendale County. They were Alex Remington's friends when the chips were down, rebuilding his trailer being a case in point, but they were also two-faced and would sell him out for a case of beer. Did he blame his fair-weather frenemies of Glendale County? No, not really, because he was a part of the fabric of Glendale County too, caught up in a world of real-life drama, in denial of human frailty, and a consequence of that.

Chapter 86

Jane Stanley studied Al Critch's business card that had been slipped under her apartment door. She had found it when she came home from grocery shopping at the local mini mart. It was Saturday afternoon. She set the grocery bags down on the kitchen countertop and dialed the number on the card. The handyman picked up on the first ring.

"What can I do you for?" Al said in his hillbilly slang.

"A general inspection," Jane Stanley said, trying to sound more confident than she felt as she studied a chipped fingernail.

"What time would be convenient for you?" Al asked, getting out his appointment book.

"I'm just putting away the groceries and then I have a hair appointment at 3:00 pm."

"I'm on call 24/7. Would 7:00 pm be too late?" Al asked officiously. He covered the receiver and took a bite of his honey crisp apple and set it down again. Some juice dribbled down his chin and he wiped it with his sleeve. Or was he drooling? Hard to be sure of anything when it came to Al, the handyman, no job too big or too small.

Purr-fect! Jane thought. "That will have to do," Jane said icily, and hung up without saying goodbye.

Chapter 87

At 7:00 pm sharp, Al Critch stood at the door of Jane Stanley's humble apartment on Valley View Drive and pressed the buzzer. She buzzed him in and was standing in the doorway when he came up the stairwell.

"My, that's a lot of tools you're carrying for a simple inspection," Jane observed.

"I came prepared," Al replied, wandering around the tiny apartment.

"Don't go in there!" Jane said frantically as she scurried over to the guest room and closed the door. "I'm afraid I don't have many guests and it's turned into my storage room." She stood with her back against the door, guarding her secrets.

"What do you have stashed in there? Snow White and the seven dwarfs?"

"My last handyman," Jane said, mustering up her best poker face. Then she swung the door open wide. If Al was shocked by Jane's macabre sense of humor, he didn't let on. There were four boxes of equal size in the middle of the floor. Otherwise the room was bare. Not even a roll-a-bed.

"What's this?" Al asked suspiciously.

"Boxes."

"I can see that."

"When I moved in, I never finished unpacking," Jane replied helplessly.

Al paused, feeling awkward. Then he cleared his throat, and spoke. "What repairs do you need done?" he asked, getting down to business.

"You're the expert. You tell me."

"Do you have any drips?"

"What's that?"

"Drips? Leaks?"

"Oh, none of that."

"Any holes in the wall that need patching up?"

"Nope."

"Any burnt out light bulbs?"

"Nope."

Al Critch was feeling more frustrated by the minute.

"There are cobwebs!" Jane blurted out indignantly. "Evidence of spiders."

"Why didn't you just say so in the first place?" Al looked at his watch, pretending he had somewhere else to go afterward and was pressed for time.

"Look, if you're too busy…"

"Do you have a broom?" Al asked, opening a closet door.

"It's in here," Jane volunteered, pulling out a broom and passing it to Al. "That's the coat closet."

Al nodded and picked up the broom. "Show me where the cobwebs are."

Jane marched over to the living room. "There!" she said triumphantly, pointing up at the ceiling.

Al reached up with the broom and brushed away the cobwebs. Then he inspected the broom for spiders. "See," he said, "there's nothing to worry about, but it you're still worried, I'll pass your broom under some hot water. That'll kill anything that moves."

"Impressive," Jane said when Al was finished. She moved closer to him. "How much do I owe you for your services?"

"I'll have to write up an estimate…a matter of routine." He pulled out his trusty clipboard, for intimidation purposes, no less, and started scribbling on it. When he was done, he read off the clipboard, "The home visit is $20, and I charge $20/hour, so that will be $40 in total."

"Forty dollars!" Jane said, practically hitting the roof. "You should have told me that up front. I'm on a fixed income. Can't you reduce your price just a little bit?"

Al took off his ball cap and scratched his balding head, using the carpenter's pencil behind his ear. He scratched behind his ear too before putting his ball cap back on and returning his carpenter's pencil to its rightful spot. He ignored Jane's outburst, and there was an awkward silence between them.

"Would you like some coffee?" Jane volunteered, filling the silence.

Al hesitated, "If it's not too much trouble."

Chapter 88

Remington sat in Myrtle's hot seat in her makeshift beauty parlor above the Five and Dime. "Hmm," she said, inspecting Remington's beaded hair. "When was the last time you washed this?" she asked, holding a greasy strand of hair between her fingers accusingly.

"Before you turned me into a black man," Remington replied smugly.

"You want these out?" Myrtle asked, playing with his beads with her long, spindly fingers.

"Cut it all off. And I mean short."

"As you wish," Myrtle replied, snipping away at the sides, one sorry-looking strand at a time. "Do you want a Mohawk?" she asked brightly.

"What's that?"

"I leave a strip of hair down the center and shave the sides."

"No thanks, ma'am. I'm tired of being the joke of the community. I want a normal haircut."

"There ain't no such thing as normal when it comes to you," Myrtle replied, wickedly holding the scissors. Remington attempted to stand up but Myrtle roughly pushed him back down. She got out the shaver.

"What are you doing?"

"Giving you a brush cut."

"I don't want a brush cut. That's too short."

"My, my, you're a hard one to please! Do it yourself!" Myrtle cackled and returned to the Five and Dime to count the daily deposit.

Alex looked in the mirror and gingerly picked up the scissors. He picked up a strand of beaded hair and snipped. The strand fell to the ground. Then he snipped another beaded strand of hair and another. When he was done, he got down on his hands and knees and picked up every blessed strand of beaded hair and put them in his pocket. He didn't trust that Myrtle wouldn't use them to put some voodoo curse on him.

Alex came down the stairs. Myrtle hissed at him like a deranged alley cat as Alex made a beeline for the door.

"That should teach you a lesson!" Myrtle snapped. Then she threw her head back and laughed.

Chapter 89

Alex walked down the sidewalk. He touched his hair. It was sticking up at weird angles like a dozen bent bastards' drunken erections. He shoved his hands in his pockets and rounded a corner, practically bowling Bunny over.

"Where's my money?" she demanded. She smelled like whiskey and perfume and weed. Alex liked the way she smelled. "You know, for the coat," she added, in case Alex had forgotten.

Alex looked confused for a moment. "Oh, that coat."

"Don't get cute with me, Mick Jagger," Bunny pouted, lighting a fresh cigarette off one that she'd just smoked down to the filter.

Alex reached in his pocket and peeled off a twenty. "Is that enough?" Bunny grabbed the twenty and shoved it in her purse. Then she held out her hand expecting more.

"Consider that a down payment," Alex said smugly. "Now if you don't mind, I'm going to the Sundance for a drink."

"Looking like that? Did Myrtle do that to you?"

"All I wanted to do was return her beads," Alex confessed, emptying his pockets. The beaded strands of hair landed on the ground and fell into a heap. Bunny laughed and her ample bosom jiggled up and down like jelly.

"Nesting material for rats," Bunny said, trying her best to console Alex, but having the opposite effect. "Consider that your good deed for the day. Come on, I'll buy you a drink," Bunny said brightly, linking arms with Alex and steering him toward the Sundance Saloon.

What the hell, at least he wasn't hog-tied in the alley this time around. And he didn't have to see his beaded hair every time he looked over his shoulder either. As a matter of fact, he was done looking over his shoulder.

"What'll it be?" Hank Lapaloosa asked.

"He'll have a *slippery nipple* and I'll have a *cockteaser*," Bunny said, licking her lips.

"I don't make fancy drinks," Hank said. He placed two rum and cokes in front of them and pulling out a fresh bowl of peanuts from behind the bar. "I have to hide the peanuts every time Detective Joe Willis comes in here. If I don't give him a real drink, he throws his ice in the peanuts. I can't very much call the cops on him, now can I?"

Alex smirked. Bunny shook her head and pulled out the twenty to pay for the drinks.

"Forget it, Bunny. The first round's on the house."

"Since when did you turn into Prince Charming?" Bunny asked Hank, batting her eyelashes.

"I've seen all kinds of things," the bartender replied. "Things that just ain't right."

"What are you, a crusader now?" Bunny asked. Hank fell silent and proceeded to wipe down the bar.

"At least you have a friend in your corner," Alex reminded Bunny and took a sip.

"Meaning you?"

"Do you need a friend?"

"Maybe I do," Bunny replied coyly, pulling out the $20 bill again for another round.

"Put that away," Alex said, gesturing to Hank for two more. He pulled out his wallet and paid for their drinks.

"Let's make a toast—*to bad haircuts!*" Bunny said, raising her glass high.

"To bad haircuts!" Alex joined in, and raised his glass even higher.

"Hold that thought," Bunny said flirtatiously. Then she slithered off her stool and sashayed over to the jukebox and fed it some quarters. "To Mick Jagger!" Bunny shouted. Alex listened to the jukebox playing in the background. It seemed as if Bunny were taunting him…"I heard a story, all about you…I heard the secrets, maybe they're true…"

Chapter 90

Jane Stanley carried an ornate tray of coffee, sugar, and cream and set it on the coffee table. Then she sat down across from Al Critch, adjusting her skirt as she did so.

"Help yourself," the perfect hostess said.

There was an awkward silence between them which seemed to last forever. Jane fidgeted with the frills on her white, see-through blouse. Nervously, she took a sip of coffee and set her cup down again.

Al thought Jane was trying to impress him—him of all people in his greasy coveralls and equally greasy unwashed hair hidden underneath his baseball cap. "If I had known this was going to be a formal affair, I'd have dressed for the occasion," Al said, lifting his hat like a gentleman from the Victorian era.

"Maybe we can work something out," Jane volunteered.

"What do you have in mind?" Al asked. He held his cup in both hands instead of by the handle, afraid to break it. Gingerly, he took a sip, which was more of an act than anything else, because usually he downed his coffee in one gulp.

"How's $10 a month sound?"

"I hate to break it to you," Al said, studying his bone china teacup and saucer, as if seeing it for the very first time, "but that won't even pay for my gas on the way over here."

Jane hung her head and looked like she was about to cry. "I just finished paying the mechanic so I can keep my car on the road," she admitted. Then the floodgates opened wide and she started bawling. In desperation, Al raced to the bathroom and came back with a wad of tissues. If there was one thing that Al Critch had a weakness for, it was a damsel in distress, and this one was pushing all the right buttons.

"Here," he said, offering Jane a tissue. "I hate to see a grown lady cry." *Even if they are crocodile tears*, he thought to himself.

Chapter 91

Bunny and Alex played some more tunes on the jukebox and then Bunny grew serious. "You can't just leave Myrtle's beads in the back alley," she said in a sober voice, looking Alex straight in the eye.

"Why not?" Alex asked, furrowing his brow like a schoolboy struggling with a difficult math problem.

"Karma. Otherwise you'll end up right back to square one."

"Oh, come on. You don't expect me to believe that crap?"

"I've been around the block a few times, Sweetie."

"No kidding."

"This isn't child's play," Bunny cautioned, her mood growing suddenly dark. "We've got to get those beads back before somebody else finds them." She made a beeline for the door and ran over to where the beaded strands of hair lay. They were already beginning to blend in with the muck and garbage that littered the back alley.

Bunny took the peanut bowl she had conveniently snatched out of her purse and emptied the peanuts onto the ground. Then she systematically removed the beads from each matted lock of hair and place them in the bowl. When she was done, she sashayed over to the Five and Dime with her sacred offering. Alex trailed after her, looking like a lost puppy, and just as mangy.

Myrtle saw the beads and grabbed the bowl. "Gimme that!" she ordered. "I have customers! Now scram!" She bent down and laboriously hid the beads under the counter before coming up for air. "And if I ever see you two in here again, I'm calling the police!" she screeched, sounding like a wounded banshee.

"Come on! Let's make a run for it!" Bunny said, laughing. They ran until their lungs felt like they were going to burst, as if a ghost from the past were chasing them. And then Alex pushed Bunny up against the wall, and pressed his body against hers. Their chests heaved in unison like they were one being with one body, but two heads.

When Bunny stopped laughing she explained Myrtle to him, like she had solved the puzzle of Myrtle that nobody else could. "Myrtle has a thing for Detective Joe Willis, so she'll call him every chance she gets. That's why you don't want to owe her."

"What about Hank Lapaloosa's peanuts and peanut bowl? Won't stealing from Hank bring you bad karma too?" Alex asked, feeling philosophical.

"I can take care of Hank," Bunny said, folding her arms. "I'll pay him back in trade. Can you do the same for Myrtle?"

Alex stepped back. "That's different," he protested.

"How so?"

"Because I'm not in love with her, so don't even go there," Alex replied.

"Do you have to be in love with somebody to screw them?" Bunny asked, genuinely mystified.

"I'm not like you."

"How so?"

"Because you'd screw everything in sight if the price was right!" Alex blurted out. Suddenly Bunny's expression changed as all hell broke loose and she began shoving him and scratching at his eyes. She pushed Alex to the ground but he twisted around and shoved Bunny's face into the mud and held her there for what seemed like an eternity.

"How does it feel to be humiliated?" Alex Remington asked. Bunny groaned and went limp and held her breath. All tricks of the trade.

Afraid he had killed Bunny, Alex suddenly released his grip and jumped off her. He felt for a pulse. "Bunny! Wake up!" Alex pleaded. "I'm so sorry…"

Unsure of what script to use next, Bunny looked up at him with dewy eyes.

"…but I'm not sorry about you," Alex added, and held her face in his two hands. He pressed his lips against Bunny's, and even though her lips were grimy with mud, he liked the way she tasted. Bunny guided Alex's hand underneath her skirt and dipped his fingers into her sugar pot.

Chapter 92

Suddenly, the back of the Sundance Saloon lit up like a Christmas tree as a car drove into the alley. "Run, Alex! That's my pimp!" Bunny shouted, as a menacing-looking man got out of the car. He was wielding a baseball bat. He hit the tip of the bat against his other hand a couple of times to let Alex know he meant business.

Bunny threw her purse as far as she could throw it. Then she fell on her knees and pointed with a trembling finger. "Help! I've been robbed!" she yelled. "He went that way!"

For a few moments, Alex froze in his tracks like a deer blinded by the headlights until he came to his senses. Then Alex ran into the Sundance Saloon and looked around. His first inclination was to run into the men's washroom but being drowned in a toilet bowl wasn't on his bucket list. So he changed course and ran into the woman's washroom instead where he got swarmed by several women who began hitting him with their purses. *The lesser of two evils,* he rationalized.

"He's after me!" Alex managed to bawl out.

"Who is?"

"Bunny's pimp!"

"I work here. Name's Joanne. You can hide in the office until things simmer down. Quick! Follow me!" Joanne barked and Alex, more than grateful, obeyed. Once inside the office, Alex fell into a heap in a chair, exhausted.

"Bring me a double vodka," Alex said, "and go send somebody to check up on Bunny."

"You've got to be kidding. If you weren't so busy thinking with your dick, you might be a little smarter on the uptake."

"What's that supposed to mean?"

"Bunny and her pimp have been conning people for years. You just got played, mister," Joanne said, giving Alex a sympathetic look.

Chapter 93

Joanne disappeared and returned a few minutes later with a double vodka. "I don't work for peanuts, John Boy," Joanne said, holding out her hand patiently.

Alex pulled out a five. "Keep the change."

"Looks like you could use the change more than me," Joanne replied, and tried to pass the change back. But Alex shook his head.

"Can you play me something on the jukebox?" Alex asked and took a swig of vodka.

"Alright, Love," Joanne said. "Just don't steal from the safe or Hank Lapaloosa will cut your fingers off." Joanne gently closed the office door and locked it. Alex took another swig of vodka and began to relax. Soon Billy Joel's, *The Piano Man* could be heard in the background.

How very fucking appropriate, Alex thought, spinning himself around in the office chair. As the room blurred, his mind became crystal clear. Knowing Bunny, however briefly, helped him figure out April. *April told me she's a party girl and that she doesn't love me. She's not much different from Bunny. It's not about me. It's about the money and drugs and booze and sex.* Stripped of my vices, I'm an unwanted man. Alex suddenly stood up on the office chair, looking like a surfer facing his waterloo.

Finally, when the room stopped spinning, Alex Remington, a reborn man, reborn in the back of a bar, no less, picked up the office phone and called the Sundance Saloon. Hank Lapaloosa picked up on the first ring. "I'll have another double vodka," Alex said cheerfully, "and a bowl of peanuts because I haven't eaten all day."

"Do you want me to run a tab?" Hank asked with growing interest.

"Not if you're going to charge me for the night," Alex replied brightly.

Who turned on his light bulb? Hank thought to himself. "It never even crossed my mind," Hank said a little too politely and hung up. He pulled out another peanut bowl from under the counter and made Alex a double vodka on the rocks.

"Bring this to the elephant in the next room," Hank said to Joanne. "And pull out the cot for him. We don't want this place turning into a circus."

Chapter 94

Maybelline paced back and forth. She didn't know what to do. The cookie jar looked like it had been moved ever so slightly, so she got out her ladder to get a closer look. That is when she discovered that the money was all there, but the gun was missing.

Maybelline picked up the phone. "We need to talk," she said to Al.

"We're talking now, aren't we?"

"In person."

"I have to mow the Periwinkle's lawn."

"You just mowed it yesterday. I could see you from my living room window."

That darn woman doesn't miss a beat, Al thought to himself. "The quack grass by the gravel driveway has to be trimmed by hand. I haven't finished the job."

"Oh," Maybelline said. "So why didn't you call me last night?"

"I was running errands. It got late."

"Since when did that stop you? Sweetheart, you know I stay up late watching Johnny Carson."

"I'm sorry, Honey. Is that what this is all about?"

"I just wanted to hear your voice, that's all," Maybelline said, feeling derailed. "You don't seem like your usual self."

"Meaning?"

"I don't know. I'm just feeling insecure, that's all."

"I have to go. The Periwinkles are expecting me."

"Come over afterward. I'll make you a carrot cake with your favorite cream cheese icing."

"I can't make any promises," Al replied, thinking about Jane Stanley's glorious cobwebs. *If I were a spider, I'd sit down beside her*, Al thought, as his mind drifted away to unchartered territory. Then, feeling guilty, Al realized that Maybelline deserved, at the very least, a decent lie. "I'm behind schedule as it is, Maybelline."

"I'll swing by the Doghouse and put the cake by the door then," Maybelline said, trying to keep disappointment out of her voice.

"Put it in the bar fridge. I don't want the ants to get first dibs."

"Okay, Sweetheart," Maybelline said and hung up. That's my Al. Always one step ahead of me, Maybelline thought, looking out the window to see what kind of day it was going to be. Then she remembered her missing gun. It was not something she wished to discuss over the phone.

Chapter 95

The Cat Lady looked out the window. Sure enough, Al was over at the Periwinkles trying his best to coax the Periwinkles' quack grass into submission with the gardening shears. She felt ashamed for thinking that Al had taken her gun. *It's a good thing that she didn't confront him*, she thought. *Relationships can be so fragile.*

Maybelline proceeded to pull out the dry ingredients for her carrot cake from the cupboards and eggs from the fridge. She used the carrots she had pulled that morning from her garden, peeling them first with a vegetable peeler before grating them. After stirring the mix into a smooth batter, Maybelline poured it into a greased and floured loaf pan. Then she placed the pan into the pre-heated oven and set the timer. When the cake was done, she brought it over to Al's place.

The latch to the Doghouse door was easy to unlatch because it was tied shut with a simple piece of twine. "Burglar proof," Al used to laugh, knowing that his reputation as a street fighter 'back in the day' preceded him. And even though the Doghouse sign read, 'Men Only', Al made an exception for Maybelline from time to time, except when it was boys' night out.

Maybelline entered the Doghouse and shut the door behind her. She put the cake in the fridge and kicked off her shoes. Maybelline resisted the urge to cut a slice of carrot cake for herself because once she went down that path there was no turning back. One slice would lead to another until she'd eaten the entire cake. Then, embarrassed and needing to save face, Maybelline would have to bake another one.

She opened the bar fridge and cracked open a beer. Then she reached over the door sill and fumbled around. She knew that Al always had an extra joint stashed up there for emergencies. Now was such a time. Maybelline always smoked alone or with Al, and only in the Doghouse. She lit the joint and inhaled deeply, then coughed. Nobody knew she liked to smoke up except Al.

The beer went down smoothly. After stubbing out her joint, Maybelline lay down on the humble cot and dozed off. When she awoke a short while later, she placed her feet on the wooden floor boards and sat up. That's strange. One of the floor boards creaked underfoot and she checked to see if it was loose. To the Cat Lady's amazement, the floor board could be easily removed to reveal a secret compartment. Reaching around inside, her fingers stumbled upon something cold to the touch. "It's my gun!" she exclaimed, cradling it in her arms.

Just then Maybelline heard footsteps outside. It sounded like someone was circling the shack, looking for a way to break in. She was glad there was no window, only a peephole in the front door.

"Who's there? The mailman?" Maybelline asked even though she knew the mail only went to Al's trailer and not to the Doghouse. Maybelline looked down at the gun she was still holding. She put a stubby finger to her lips in a "Shh!" gesture that only Dear God could see and put the muzzle of the gun to the peephole. Coincidently, at that very instant, Al Critch put his eyeball up to the peephole.

"Stay where you are or I'll shoot!" Maybelline shouted and slowly pulled the trigger. Al felt a burst of water squirt into his eyeball and it stung like Hell. It stung so much that he did a little jig in a circle and fell over.

"Is that any way to court a lady?" Maybelline asked, opening the Doghouse door and slowly lowering the squirt gun. "I used this to train the cats to keep them off the countertops when I was baking," Maybelline explained apologetically. She stepped outside the Doghouse with a beer in each hand and passed one to Al. The other one she took for herself.

"I thought the gun was real," Al said, taking a swig of beer. "I took it so Belinda Jane wouldn't get hurt, seeing that you babysit for the *little squirt.*"

"How did you think to look up there?" Maybelline asked, nursing her beer.

"Alex came over to the Doghouse one night and started shooting his mouth off about you having a gun. I just had to be sure. That's all."

"That's ridiculous."

"I don't think Alex knew you had a gun, fake or otherwise. I think he just concocted the story to get the simple folks of Glendale County all worked up. Worked, didn't it?"

Maybelline pondered this a moment, then she flung the fake gun as far as she could.

"I'm sure there's a lesson in there somewhere, or maybe a sermon," Al said, putting a loving arm around Maybelline as they stared up at the tangerine sky. "Come on, Sweet Pea, let's go back inside and try some of your delicious carrot cake."

Chapter 96

Mary Anne knocked on Professor West's office door. There was no answer. "Come on. I know you're in there," Mary Anne shouted, knocking louder and more persistently. "If you don't open up, I'm going to get Peter Carmichael to climb a tree so you'll have to come out of your isolation chamber to rescue him."

"My, you do have a way with words," the Professor said seductively as he opened the door. "Welcome to my humble little abode. Do sit down," he instructed, loosening his necktie. "Just fling the unmentionables aside." He was referring to the underwear strewn about the room. Mary Anne plopped herself down and looked around.

"What is this? Were you doing a striptease or did you fire the cleaning lady?" Mary Anne asked.

"Neither, I'm just a dirty, old bachelor. Besides, nobody comes here when I'm between classes, so this is quite a surprise."

"Just checking up on you, that's all. Oh, by the way, Alex Remington got his hair cut. No more beads. Looks like he cut it himself," Mary Anne added, blocking out the silence by mindless chatter.

"Devil may care," Professor West said dismissively, reaching for the flask in his desk drawer and pouring himself a stiff one. "I've cut back," he added, as if that made any difference.

"Oh, that's a shame," Mary Anne replied, "because I've stepped it up a notch."

"*Notch?* What a curious word coming from you. Makes me think of a bedpost with notches carved into it, signifying sexual conquests. Is that what brought you here, Mary Anne? The possibility of a sexual conquest?"

Mary Anne's jaw dropped. No words fell out.

"Coffee then?" Professor West offered. "Where are my manners?" He proceeded to plug in the electric kettle sitting on the windowsill and took out

2 cups, a jar of instant coffee, coffee whitener and sugar cubes. "Tell me," the Professor said, half turning to face Mary Anne, "Did you really think that you could convince Peter Carmichael to climb up a tree, if all else failed, to get me to open the door?"

"It worked though, didn't it? Because here I am in all my glory," Mary Anne said with a lop-sided grin.

"I just didn't like the idea of Peter damaging a tree. I was an activist in the Sixties."

"Oh," Mary Anne said, looking down at the carpet. Something tucked away in the far corner caught her eye. *Was it a condom or an elastic band?* She couldn't say for sure. She took a deep breath. "I missed you, you big old whack job."

"That's the nicest thing that anybody has ever said to me in a very long time," Professor West said, conscientiously straightening the papers on his desk.

"I see you still have an office. When's the next class?"

"I'm on sabbatical so I can write my book," Professor West said. The kettle was whistling and he got up to unplug it. "How do you like your coffee?"

"Black with a bit of sugar," Mary Anne said. The Professor drank his coffee black too, but with a splash of whiskey, no sugar. "What's the book about?"

"You'll have to come to my book signing," the Professor said. "Why spoil it?"

"Where is this book signing going to be?"

"I haven't worked out the details yet."

The devil's in the details, Mary Anne thought. And for the first time she saw past Professor West's aristocratic snobbishness and she liked what she saw.

Chapter 97

Al Critch was a man with a conscience and right now he was wrestling with what he was going to do about Jane Stanley. He decided to tell her the truth and picked up the phone. "We have to talk," he said.

"Is it about the $40 dollars? You're not going to put me in the Collection Agency or break my legs, are you?" Jane asked.

"No, I'll get somebody else to do my dirty work. When are you going to be home so I can send over my goons?"

"You can't be serious?" Jane asked, turning on the kitchen tap and pouring herself a glass of water.

"No, Jane. I was joking. And it's not about the money either. When are you free?"

"This afternoon."

"Great. How about I swing by your place within the next hour or so?"

"Now you've got me worried," Jane said. "If it's not about the money and you can't tell me over the phone, what exactly is this about?"

"You'll have to trust me on this one Jane, okay?"

"Okay. I'll see you when you get here," Jane said and hung up. She popped a valium. *Take occasionally. When stressed.* She was stressed now. As the valium began to take effect, she started to feel paranoid. *Al Critch can see right through me*, she thought. It wasn't about the cobwebs at all and he knew it. She was lonely. And now he was going to blow her off, politely, of course, which made it all the more dreadful.

Chapter 98

Just then, there was a knock on the door. It came sooner than expected. Jane straightened her skirt and faced the music. "Who is it?" she asked, knowing that it was likely Al Critch on the other side of the door.

"It's me. Al. Open up." Jane let the handyman in and locked the door behind him.

"Where are your tools?" Jane asked suspiciously.

"In the truck."

"So, why're you here?" Jane asked, trying not to slur her words, unsure where this was going.

"There's no easy way to put it," Al Critch said. "I haven't been perfectly honest with you. Maybe you'd better have a seat."

"We'll sit in the kitchen. Coffee?"

"No, just a glass of water will do." Jane poured a glass of water for Al and set it down in front of him. Al took an obligatory sip. Then he looked Jane straight in the eye as she sat at the kitchen table across from him. She looked so dignified that he questioned if he was doing the right thing. And then he thought of Maybelline and her carrot cake. A woman with a heart of gold. Jane had lured him down the garden path away from the straight and narrow and admittedly he had been tempted, except divine intervention in the form of carrot cake and a water pistol had brought him to his senses.

"There's never going to be an us," Al blurted out, "shifting uneasily in his chair. And you can forget about the $40 dollars because after I leave here, I'm not coming back." Al waited several minutes for what he'd just said to sink in, before continuing. "You need to find somebody for yourself just like I have Maybelline."

"Is that it? Are you through?" Jane snapped angrily.

"Jane, you need to hire a cleaning lady to take care of your cobweb problem."

"What? Are you saying that I'm not clean?"

"A cleaning lady is cheaper."

"Are you mocking me?"

Al felt cornered. The whole truth might hurt Jane more, but she'd get over it faster than if he strung her along with little white lies and half-truths to let her down gently. *You have to be cruel to be kind*, he thought, and decided to spill the beans about Thomas, come Hell or high water. He put his glass in the kitchen sink, playing the role of the perfect gentleman, and moved toward the door.

Al turned to face Jane, "Oh, and by the way. Thomas across the hall doesn't like to be bugged for coffee and sugar all the time."

"Doesn't like to be bugged?" Jane asked, growing angrier by the minute.

"Thomas hired me," Al said, "to fix his little problem," and he made parenthesis with his fingers for emphasis.

"Meaning me?" Jane asked. Tears streamed down her cheeks as awareness suddenly kicked in, twinning with the valium. All willed himself out of the apartment and down the stairs. He jumped into his truck and squealed out of the parking lot.

I'm a handyman, not a shrink. How do I end up in these situations anyway? he asked himself. At the next intersection, he pulled a joint down from the visor and sparked it up. Then he drove straight over to Maybelline's. She opened the screen door before he even got out of his truck. I'm going to earn that fine lady, Al thought to himself, skipping up the steps and giving Maybelline a heart-felt squeeze.

"Is there such a thing as male menopause?" Maybelline asked herself as she melted in his loving arms.

Chapter 99

Marjorie picked a slot machine and sat down. As usual she squeezed her lucky rabbit's foot, scrunched her eyes, and prayed. "Good luck, Mother," Mary Anne said encouragingly before going to the bar for her usual espresso.

"What's up?" Mary Anne asked Thomas when she sat down.

"Plenty," Thomas said. "Jane Stanley found out the truth about why Al Critch's business card was slipped under her door."

"Who told her?"

"Al did."

"But why?"

"Beats me," Thomas said, and shrugged. He placed a tiny cup of steaming espresso in front of Mary Anne.

"Maybe Al is not the hound dog we thought he was," Mary Anne commented.

"What's that supposed to mean?"

"What it means," Mary Anne said, sounding both noble and wise, "is that we thought Al and Jane Stanley would end up having an affair. Ergo, no more knocks on your door for sugar. Problem solved."

"Problem solved alright but now every time Jane passes me in the hallway she gives me the cold shoulder. She won't even say hi."

"Careful what you ask for," Mary Anne cautioned, keeping an eye on her mother. "What did you expect for Jane to say, 'Thank you Thomas for breaking up with me before our first date'?"

Thomas looked thoughtful. "In retrospect, I should have told Jane I'm out of sugar or coffee or whatever from the get-go, or not even answered the door. She might have taken a hint. The last thing I wanted to do was hurt Jane's feelings," Thomas confessed.

"She'll get over it."

"You think?"

"No."

"That helps," Thomas sighed, then tended to a lonely woman at the other end of the counter. *An admirer?* Mary Anne wondered.

Marjorie came into the lounge just then and tapped her daughter on the shoulder.

Mary Anne turned around. "Any luck?" she asked.

"Not tonight, but at least I didn't lose my shirt."

"Maybe we need to get you another rabbit's foot," Mary Anne suggested. "Yours is looking a little raggedy."

"Nah, if the machine's going to pay out, it's going to pay out. Bad timing, that's all," Marjorie said matter-of-factly.

"Don't you believe in luck anymore? Or fate? Or prayers?"

"I only believe in luck and fate and prayers when I win. When I lose, I don't believe in anything."

"You're trying to get the machines to decide your *'deservedness'*," Mary Anne said. "That's why you gamble."

"*Deservedness*? I've never heard of anything so preposterous."

"By gambling with your *deservedness* and putting it on the line, you are guaranteed to set yourself up for disappointment most of the time," Mary Anne said, suddenly the expert on such matters.

Marjorie slowly reached for her drink.

"No wonder you drink, Mother."

Marjorie was about to take a sip, but hesitated because what her daughter had just said hit her like a ton of bricks. "Is this what they're teaching you at the college these days? How to psychoanalyze your own mother?"

"Class has been out for weeks, Marjorie. Where have you been?"

"I've been watching Erno jog around the neighborhood making a fool out of us."

"Is that what you think?"

Marjorie grabbed Mary Anne's arm and leaned in closer. "It's what I know," she said.

"It's worse than I thought," Mary Anne said to herself. "I think maybe it's time to go home," Mary Anne suggested, putting on her sweater and gathering up her purse.

"Speak for yourself, Mary Anne. Because I'm not going anywhere." Marjorie had that look in her eye that said, "Don't challenge me or there will be consequences."

"I can't just leave you here."

"And why not, Spoil Sport? I'm old enough to drink and gamble."

"Suit yourself," Mary Anne said. "Call me when you're ready to come home."

"You're not going to just leave her here, are you?" Thomas asked. "I mean, isn't your mother a bit—?"

"—senile?" Marjorie interrupted. "Isn't that what you were going to say?"

Bartending 101: The customer's always right. But in this case, it doesn't help, Thomas thought uneasily.

Chapter 100

"Would you like a drink on the house?" Thomas asked Marjorie, trying to save face.

"Only if you insist."

"I insist."

"Oh, alright then. Where's Mary Anne?"

"She just left."

"Without me?"

"You said you wanted to stay. Mary Anne wants you to call her when you're ready to come home."

"Pass me the phone."

"Mary Anne just left. She's probably not even home yet."

"Why didn't you try to stop her?"

"It's not my place to—"

"—Oh, I see. You're just a bartender," Marjorie snapped.

Thomas said nothing. *If in doubt, hold thy tongue.*

"Don't let it happen again or you're fired!" Marjorie scolded. Underneath all that anger it was clear that Marjorie had abandonment issues.

"I'm right here," Thomas said reassuringly, "and I'm not going anywhere."

"Boy, you're cute," Marjorie said flirtatiously, suddenly changing gears. "What's your name?"

"Don't you remember?"

"You're George."

Thomas searched the *Bartender* roll-a-desk in his mind for the right answer. "George, that's me. That's my name. Don't wear it out!"

Thomas quietly dialed Mary Anne's number from the phone under the counter. "You'd better come get your mother. I'm not a babysitter," he said in a barely audible whisper.

"First you call me senile. Then you call me a baby. What do you think I have? Early onset dementia?" Marjorie asked. She was furious.

"No, but that machine over there looks like it's about to pay out," Thomas said, slipping her a $10 bill. Marjorie shook her head and gave Thomas a conspiratorial wink before scurrying over to the machine. Out came the sacred rabbit's foot.

"You're supposed to blow on it," said an old man playing the slot machine next to her.

"You should be ashamed of yourself!" Marjorie said sternly and put the rabbit's foot back in her purse.

Chapter 101

What Marjorie was suffering from was neither dementia nor alcoholism, the Dollhouse ladies decided, but neglect, so they decided to turn their usual Dollhouse get-together into spa night, especially for her.

Mary Anne dropped Marjorie off and helped her down from the Chevy. The Dollhouse ladies helped Marjorie inside. "Bye Mother," Mary Anne shouted and blew her mother a kiss. Marjorie puckered her lips and blew but what came out sounded more like a fart than a kiss. Or maybe it was the Chevy backfiring.

Once inside, Bella invited Marjorie to lie back in the chaise lounge and Sandy Brosben began prepping Marjorie's feet. She wrapped them in steaming towels for 15 minutes. Then she put sponge wedges between Marjorie's toes and clipped her toenails. When she was finished, she brought out a tray of different colors of nail polish. There was ruby red, emerald green, tangerine orange, and metallic gold.

"I'll have metallic gold," Marjorie said excitedly. "It'll go with my sequined shawl."

As Sandy patiently painted Marjorie's toenails, Bella made a face mask out of honey and oatmeal. Then she put a slice of cucumber over each eye. "That'll remove the puffiness."

"What difference does it make? Erno doesn't notice me anyway," Marjorie said, fidgeting with a tissue in her lap and balling it up in her fists.

"You're not getting beautified for Erno," Bella said.

"I'm not?"

"You're getting this done for you."

"I am?"

"Why, of course, Dear. This is ladies' night out and we're going to turn you into a lady." Bella's hand suddenly shot up to her mouth. *Did I just say that*, she thought, squeezing her eyes tightly shut, as if she was trying, through paranormal channels, to take it back.

"What she means," Sandy interjected, "coming to Bella's rescue, is that we're here to bring out the *real* you."

"Honey and oatmeal…tar and feathers…I can't tell the difference," Marjorie said. The truth was that Marjorie wasn't happy unless she was complaining.

Jane Stanley was in charge of the ambience. She chose soothing music and sandalwood incense and dollar store candles. Marjorie couldn't tell if it was spa music or funeral music, or if it was sandalwood or marijuana, but whatever it was, it was working.

Then the devil got the upper hand and Marjorie removed one of her cucumber slices, and spoke, "Are you over your cobwebs?" Marjorie asked Jane, her eyes narrowing.

"How do you know about my cobwebs? Jesus Christ! Does the whole town know?"

"Look, if it's any consolation," Bella said, an expert on such matters, "it doesn't even rate as an affair because nothing was flung, right?"

"What difference does that make to the diehard gossipers?" Jane Stanley asked, shaking the ice cubes in her empty glass.

"We all have ghosts in our closet, and cobwebs for that matter," Bella said sagely. "None of us are perfect." Bella wrapped a comforting arm around Jane.

"Marjorie, are you ready for your massage?" Maybelline asked, entering the room.

"I have brittle bone disease," Marjorie said. "What feels good to some people could land me in the hospital."

"Okay, Little China Doll," Bella teased, "time to get up and join the party before we run out of cocktail umbrellas." She brought the sandalwood incense with her as she stepped out onto the patio, followed by the Dollhouse ladies.

Chapter 102

The next morning, Marjorie awoke feeling chilly so she pulled the blankets up around herself. But when she looked down at her exposed toes, she began to scream. "Quick, Erno, fetch my eyeglasses!" Erno found them on the night stand and put them on Marjorie's face, careful not to tangle them up in her hair which was full of curlers.

"What happened to your toenails?" Erno asked incredulously.

"Beats me."

"When did this happen?"

Marjorie looked like she was constipated, as she struggled to make sense of it all. "I must have blacked out," was all she said.

"You could not have done this," Erno said, horrified.

Then Marjorie began to remember Spa night at the Dollhouse, and smiled to herself, secretly enjoying Erno's newfound interest and jealousy.

Chapter 103

"What's all the commotion about?" Mary Anne asked, tapping lightly on the bedroom door which was slightly ajar.

"Marjorie's toenails."

"What about Marjorie's toenails?" Mary Anne asked, not daring to step into their sacred domain without permission. "Do you need them trimmed?"

"Too late. Come in," Marjorie said, grabbing a pillow to prop herself up.

Mary Anne bravely pushed the door open and then her jaw dropped. "Wow, Mother! Your toenails are beautiful. Where can I sign up?"

"At the Dollhouse. It was Spa Night," Marjorie replied, feeling more confident by the minute.

"Mother, I'm so very proud of you," Mary Anne said, tears welling up in her eyes.

"Bella said I needed a beauty makeover to bring out the real me. Jane Stanley was there too. Did you know about her cobwebs?" Marjorie asked Mary Anne, testing the gossip trail.

"Cobwebs? Jane Stanley?"

"Apparently Maybelline's Al was over at Jane's inspecting her apartment for cobwebs."

"And?"

"I wasn't there," Marjorie shot back, swinging her legs to the side of the bed and putting on her slippers and housecoat. Mary Anne passed Marjorie her cane. "Drop it!" Marjorie ordered, standing up. Mary Anne did as she was told and let go of the cane just as Marjorie reached for it. The frail, old woman suddenly leaned to the side and then fell back down again. Luckily the mattress was there to break her fall.

"Mother! Are you alright?" Mary Anne asked, rushing to her mother's side.

"I didn't mean drop my cane, Ding Bat! I meant drop the subject about Jane Stanley's cobwebs!"

"Maybelline's my friend too," Mary Anne said. "If he's having an affair with Jane Stanley, I think I have a right to know."

"Well he ain't. Bella Porter said it didn't qualify as an affair because *nothing was flung*."

"Maybe I should start attending those Dollhouse meetings to keep myself in the loop."

"That'd be no fun," Marjorie said, standing up and using the cane and night stand for support, "because then we wouldn't be able to talk about you."

"You can't be serious," Mary Anne said, taken aback.

"Why, do you think we gossip about everybody except you?"

"And what do the Dollhouse Ladies say about Professor West and me?" Mary Anne asked, not knowing if her paranoia was justified.

"Everyone knows you're a wallflower," Marjorie said, touching the peeling wallpaper sympathetically as if she was caressing Mary Anne's youthful face. "They just don't know how long it's going to take for you to become unglued."

Chapter 104

Al Critch loved gardening. Every chance he got, he was down on all fours with a trowel in his hand working among his beloved flower beds. No two landscaped homes looked alike. Beneath Bella Porter's white, shuttered picture window, Al planted a variety of different colors of hollyhocks, from pink and yellow to purplish-blue and white. Around Maybelline Levine's trailer he planted different types of roses, to reflect his love for her. And for the Periwinkles, he put in a small garden.

"I have to feed my flock," Preacher Periwinkle would say. Al managed to persuade the Periwinkles to let him plant a few flowers and shrubs around the weeping willow in their front yard too. He planted anything that required filtered light.

"If only dandelions are going to grow there, then it's God's will," Al Critch told the Reverend.

"So be it!" Reverend Periwinkle said, after consulting with God on such holy matters.

But when it came to the Federno's, Marjorie would have none of it. "I don't want the handyman prowling around our trailer all hours of the day and night like an alley cat in heat!" She scolded.

"But Mother, don't you see how beautiful the other trailer lots look?" Mary Anne pleaded.

"Okay, he can plant a few tulips along the front of the property, just to deter any would-be trespassers," Marjorie said begrudgingly, feeling outnumbered.

"You can't sit in the window and guard the flowers all the time," Mary Anne scolded gently.

"Yeah. Mary Anne's right," Erno said. "Do you really think that trespassers have a conscience when it comes to trampling on flowers?"

Chapter 105

Dino Miskatorus loved his quaint little diner. It put Glendale County on the map. Tourists as far as Florida had wandered into his tiny little diner and were amazed by his heaping platefuls of pasta and delicious homemade pies. On the wall in Dino's office was a group picture of all the staff—Mary Anne, Wendy, Maybelline, Al, and of course, himself. Dino's Diner did not have a set closing time. "If it's busy, we stay open. Business is business," he would say in his thick European accent.

One evening in the middle of summer, a tour bus from Regina stopped for a snack and washroom break. One washroom, two stalls, 40 tourists having to pee. The lineup was so long that Dino was worried that somebody in the line was going to 'wet their drawers'. "That would be very bad for business," he explained, so he let the tourists use the staff washroom too. The queue was promptly divided into two lineups that had to be skillfully navigated by customers as they went to pay their bill. Fortunately, the tourists all ordered sandwiches and coffee to go. "Make them all ham and Swiss with mayo. No substitutions," Dino ordered Mary Anne who was called in on short notice.

Al Critch and Maybelline were called in too to help out. They formed an assembly line. The bread slices were lined up, tops and bottoms, by Dino himself. Al put the ham and Swiss on the bottom slice of bread. Mary Anne put a dollop of mayo on the top slice, then closed the sandwiches and wrapped each one with saran wrap. Finally, Maybelline put each completed sandwich in a brown paper bag with a single napkin.

Dino's staff stood outside smiling and waving as the tourists boarded the bus. "Y'all come back, ya hear!" Al shouted gleefully, but Mary Anne gave him a quick poke in the ribs.

"You can't say that. They'll think we're Americans," she said crisply.

"What's wrong with that?" Al asked innocently, still waving foolishly, even after the bus was long gone.

"We don't want to offend anyone in Dixieland."

Al looked up at the constellation in the night sky, then spat on the ground. "Hello? They're from Regina. If they're going to come back, it's because they like us, the food, the hospitality, Dino, the prices, the washrooms, the whole nine yards," he said philosophically, then added, "I was just being myself."

"You know what? You're right, Al. I like you just the way you are." Mary Anne put a comforting arm around Al's waist like they were about to do a line dance and steered him back toward Dino's diner. "I have a feeling that they'll be back," Mary Anne said smiling. "And don't forget your hammer underneath the counter. Eh?"

Chapter 106

Whenever Marjorie sent Mary Anne out for a beer run, Erno went out for a jog. "To resist temptation," he told Nancy Gilmoss, who spotted Erno out jogging, honked her horn, and promptly pulled over.

"I'm just being neighborly," Nancy said reassuringly. "No worries."

"I gave that up too," Erno said, lying through his false teeth.

"Gave what up? Worrying?" Nancy asked, checking her appearance in her rear-view mirror.

"Yeah, Peter's shrink says worrying's maladaptive behavior."

"Did Peter's shrink cure Peter of worrying?" Nancy asked with growing interest.

"Absolutely. She told Peter that worry clutters the mind and that a person can learn how to declutter their mind, sort of like housekeeping."

"Housekeeping?" Nancy asked, surprised at herself to be discussing housekeeping with a married man.

"You look at what you worry about and try to come up with a solution to stop worrying. Then you apply that solution."

"Can you give me an example because I'm more confused than ever," Nancy said innocently.

"Gladly. Marjorie worries about trespassers trampling on the tulip fence."

"Tulip fence?"

"Bear with me."

"I'm not going to ask you to spell that," the fifth grade English teacher said.

"Huh?"

"Oh, never mind. Go on."

"Marjorie worries about her tulips being trampled on and I worry about Marjorie worrying."

"How'd you stop?"

"I just took a mental vacation. If it happens, it happens, and I can't control that or what Marjorie might do if her tulip fence is breached."

"Breached?"

"If this, our security system, is compromised."

Geesh! Nancy thought. "Do not laugh," she told herself. "Well, my dear, I've got to get to the supermarket before all the specials are snatched up."

"Snatch while the snatching's good!" Erno said cheerfully and resumed jogging.

Chapter 107

Hank Lapaloosa put the sign on the door of the Sundance Saloon—Closed for Private Function. It was a party thrown for Troy and Lisa to celebrate their upcoming wedding. Not only was Glendale's Senior football team invited, but also their girlfriends, so the crowd was expected to be huge.

Joanne helped Hank push the tables together to form 2 long rows of end-to-end tables. Each table was covered with a red tablecloth and a white candle was placed in the center of each table. On the bar were several bowls of munchies, ranging from potato chips and cheezies to pretzels and mixed nuts. A small table sporting a white table cloth was at the end of the bar for the punch bowl. Joanne personally made the punch using Hawaiian Fruit punch mix and white rum. Pineapple and orange slices floated around in the punch bowl. To complete her masterpiece, she added a jar of maraschino cherries and crushed ice.

A postage-sized dance floor was cordoned off for the diehard rock and rollers. Up on stage, The Rubber Banditos were tuning their instruments and practicing songs that Troy and Lisa had picked out.

"You aren't pregnant, are you?" Jerry Thornapple asked Lisa.

"No, of course not," Lisa answered.

"Then we can't play, *They call it a trap.*"

There was a pregnant pause which seemed to go on forever.

"How about we play *Muskrat Love* instead?" Jerry finally suggested.

Lisa was busy making balloons and stringing them together. "Nah, how about *99 Red Balloons*?"

The Rubber Banditos started to pick out the chords. "Yeah, I think we can play it," Jerry said, nodding to the band members. He adjusted his black bandana. *So what if it sounds like a jam session*, Jerry Thornapple thought to himself. *They're not going to know the difference when they're three sheets to the wind.*

Chapter 108

Around 8:00 that evening, the partyers started pouring in. Some of the senior football players wore their jerseys to let people know who they were. There was a cover charge at the door. Drinks were paid for using tickets which were purchased from the bartender. Half of the money raised went to Troy and Lisa for their wedding and honeymoon and the other half went to the staff and the Rubber Banditos. Mary Anne showed up with Maybelline and they greeted the groom and bride-to-be.

"Jerry wasn't kidding when he said you invited the entire senior football team," Mary Anne said to Troy as she sampled some punch.

"Not only that," Troy replied, "but football players from other years keep showing up here wearing their jerseys and showing off their girlfriends' little black dresses. What am I supposed to do?"

"That's Hank Lapaloosa's problem, not yours," Maybelline replied, fishing around in the punch bowl for a maraschino cherry.

"You look like you could use a refill," Joanne said, taking Maybelline's empty punch glass and replacing it with a full one.

The Banditos played Nothing but a Hound Dog, Southern Nights, You're the One that I want, and several others before they took a break to sample the punch and mingle. They sat with the football players who were hollering like they were out on the field. One fellow got up on the table with a football in his hand. He turned around and bent over.

"Oh my God, he's going to do it!" Mary Anne exclaimed, putting a hand over her mouth. Sure enough, the football was tossed out between his legs as other football players scrambled up on the tables and tackled each other for the football.

Hank Lapaloosa grabbed the microphone just then and pulled out his ukulele. He started strumming and singing loudly to divert the guests' attention. It worked. The merrymakers started clapping and the football players surprisingly returned to their seats. "Don't cry over spilt candle wax," Joanne said nervously, drinking one glass of punch after another off her tray.

The Rubber Banditos returned to the stage and tried to coax Hank to join them with his ukulele but, much to their relief, he bowed out. The evening ended with a 50/50 draw for cash prizes and gifts, such as a TV, a bottle of champagne, and movie passes.

After Hank made the raffle announcements, he called Troy Pickett and Lisa Conway up on stage. "These two darling lovebirds," he said, giving them both a big hug, "are getting married in Vegas by Elvis!" After hearing this, everybody started cheering and clapping.

The Rubber Banditos started playing another set that included *99 Red Balloons and Don't Step on My Suede Shoes*. Suddenly the postage-sized dance floor disappeared as dancers, looking for a place to dance, sprawled up onto the stage. Somebody grabbed a string of balloons which were trampled underfoot and began popping unceremoniously.

"Quick, let's duck out the back alley," Jerry Thornapple said and Jerry and the band made a run for it. Hours later, at 3:00 in the morning, music could still be heard from the alley as a busker, looking to make some quick cash, serenaded the dwindling crowd. *They call it a trap, I can't walk out, because I love you too much baby…*

Chapter 109

"Hop in!" Nancy Gilmoss ordered with a sultry tilt of her head and a coquettish smile.

"I can't. I'm jogging," Erno replied, determined to stick to his exercise routine. It was bright and early on a Saturday morning in early July. Traffic was starting to pick up. Still others were headed to their part-time jobs.

"There is a beautiful walking trail in Cedar Falls that leads right to the Falls. It's a tourist attraction. What do you say?"

"How long is this going to take?"

"Let's make a day of it. It'll be fun."

"I have to call Marjorie first."

"What, you're going to tell her you're going to Cedar Falls just like that?"

"Just like that."

"Are you going to tell Marjorie that I'm taking you too?" Nancy asked.

"Of course. I don't drive. Marjorie's likely to get suspicious."

"There's a phone at Dino's. You can call her from there. Hop in before I change my mind."

Erno got in the passenger seat after adjusting it to make more leg room. He put on his seat belt and looked straight ahead. When they pulled up to Dino's Diner, Erno spotted Mary Anne's Chevy. "I can't call from there," he said. "What will Mary Anne think? Or the customers? They have big ears, and even bigger mouths."

Nancy pondered this a minute and then replied, "I'll go in and call Mary Anne outside and tell her. She'll see you sitting in the truck anyway."

"Alright," Erno said. He looked down at his hands and spread his fingers, then rested them in his lap and looked away.

Nancy pulled her car in front of Mary Anne's Chevy and got out. She caught Mary Anne's attention through the window and gestured for her to come to the door.

Mary Anne poked her head out. "Can't you see I'm busy?"

"I won't keep you long. Erno wants me to take him to Cedar Falls to see the Falls. I'll bring him back in one piece. Promise. Let Marjorie know he's in good hands."

"A lot of good that will do," Mary Anne said.

"Oh, I think the fresh air will do Erno a world of good," Nancy exclaimed brightly.

"No, I meant telling Marjorie. She'll have a conniption."

"Erno's a grown man. He's big enough to make his own decisions," Nancy pointed out.

"Then Erno will just have to tell Marjorie himself because I won't lie for him," Mary Anne said, and went back to serving tables. "Nobody's asking you to lie!" Nancy shouted after her.

"What'd she say?" Erno asked when Nancy got back to the truck.

"Have fun!"

Chapter 110

Professor West decided to go swimming at the pond in Cedar Falls. He packed a beach bag with swimming trunks, a beach towel, sunscreen, and his customary flask of whiskey. 'To keep away the skeeters' was his excuse.

He knew the back roads from Glendale to Cedar Falls like the back of his hand so, as a crow flies, he zig-zagged across the trusty back roads and popped out at a T-intersection with a sign indicating Bullhead Narrows to the right and Cedar Falls to the left.

When he got to the swimming hole, he changed in the car, took off his watch, and locked up. He wrapped his towel around his waist and walked in his sandals along the sandy beach until he found a suitable spot to spread out his beach towel. Then he sat down and pulled out his flask.

He watched a toddler playing in the sand. His proud parents helped him build a sandcastle and then took some pictures. The sandcastle had a moat and a drawbridge or was it the whiskey playing tricks on him. He walked over to get a closer look.

"Is that a drawbridge?" Professor *Extraordinaire* asked. The bewildered parents looked at him like he had 3 heads. "If you have a moat," Professor West explained, "you have to have a drawbridge." Just then the toddler started to cry and the young mother lifted him up in her lap to comfort him.

"Is this man bothering you?" a man behind Professor West asked, and pretty soon there was a gang of men circling him, four in total.

"I asked them for directions to The Falls," Professor West explained.

"Is that true?" the lead thug asked the toddler's father.

Not wanting to cause a commotion and spoil their outing, the toddler's mother was the first to speak. "The Falls is that way, on the other side of the pond. You have to take Beach Road East." Professor West nodded gratefully and the gang reluctantly stepped aside. Not sure if trouble was going to follow him, he decided to keep on walking and circle back for his towel and car later.

He walked some distance and then waded into the water. It felt soothing and the water smelled like lake trout, but he didn't mind. He liked trout. It reminded him of when he went fishing with his father a long, long time ago. *A lifetime ago*, the Professor thought, feeling a twinge of melancholy.

After what seemed like a reasonable length of time, the Professor strolled, as only a drunk could, back to his towel and back to his car. He worried about sand crabs, but only briefly as he turned onto Beach Road East. He'd heard about the Falls. Sometimes there was a rainbow if you were lucky and you could make a wish. Suddenly, that's all he wanted to do, make it to the Falls.

Chapter 111

Bugsy's Garage was busy with tourists and the locals who came in for their regular tune up. "If Bugsy Junior referred you, you get a discount," Bugsy Senior would say. The size of the discount varied from 10% to 50% depending on how well business was doing or if Bugsy liked you.

"How come Bugsy Junior doesn't come work for you?" Tom Jenkins asked.

"Junior doesn't want to be a grease monkey like his old man."

"He could come stock shelves at the liquor store," Tom suggested, "when he comes of age, of course."

"That won't be for another year. Say, there's hot coffee if you want some," Bugsy said, wiping his greasy hands on a rag.

"If the coffee's anything like the coffee at the Five and Dime in Bullhead Narrows, I'll pass," Myrtle Merryweather said, quivering at the thought as her ample bosom quivered right along with her. She shot Tom Jenkins a sideways glance. "What are you staring at?" Tom didn't know what to say much less know what color to turn. He settled on red. Beet red. Then he closed his eyes, hung his head, and prayed.

Chapter 112

The morning after the party came much too soon. Hank had left the Sundance just the way it was with glass on the floor and balloons and streamers scattered about like a cyclone had swept through the place. Some of the tablecloths had made their way to the floor and been trampled on. Pretzels and chips were strewn everywhere and several chairs had toppled over.

"We have a lot of cleaning up to do before 11:00 am," Hank said to Joanne as he pulled the covers off her. "*Up and at 'em,* as the saying goes." Joanne rolled over on her stomach and pulled the blankets up over her head like a turtle and groaned.

"Why don't we call maid service?" Joanne asked, emerging a few minutes later from under her blanket. "Or Al Critch? There's a business card on the dresser."

A few minutes later, Al Critch was bouncing along on the highway in his old battered truck headed to Bullhead Narrows with a motley crew bouncing around in the back of the cab, anybody he could round up on short notice. There was Bugsy Junior and Alex Remington. Peter Carmichael came along too because his shrink said he needed to 'show some initiative'.

"Cleaner than a baby's ass," Al said when they were done.

Hank opened the cash register and peeled off a few bills. "Here," he said, and Joanne brought out a box of leftover potato chips and pop.

"Just put it in the back of the truck," Al said to Joanne. "I've got to get over to mow the Periwinkle's quack grass before Mrs. Periwinkle quacks up." Al pumped the air with his elbows, imitating a duck. Hank and Joanne both laughed at the handyman's antics, but Peter's face twisted up like a question mark. He wondered what the Periwinkles had to do with his quack, but he let it go. He'd have something to talk about during his next therapy session.

Chapter 113

Lisa Conway's father closed the hardware store for the day so he could drive Troy and Lisa to the airport. Lisa had packed so many bags that she had difficulty closing the trunk.

"How long are you going for?" Mr. Conway asked. "By the looks of all that luggage, it looks like you're never coming back."

Lisa laughed. "Don't worry, Daddy."

"I'll take good care of her, Mr. Conway," Troy said reassuringly. He went to the back of the car, rearranged some luggage, and closed the trunk easily. "See, nothing to it."

They drove to Regina International Airport to catch a direct flight to Las Vegas. Father, Daughter, and soon-to-be Son-in-law hugged good-bye and soon Lisa and Troy were in the air. "Look at all the tiny houses!" Lisa exclaimed enthusiastically. "It looks like Mr. Roger's neighborhood."

"Look!" Troy said pointing. "You can see the houses with the outdoor swimming pools. They're the little blue dots."

An airline stewardess wearing a navy A-line skirt and matching blazer came to the front of the plane and announced possible turbulence and what to do in case of an emergency. She did the little demonstration with the pull-down oxygen mask and barf bag.

"Are you afraid of flying?" Lisa asked cautiously as the plane hit a little turbulence.

"No, I'm afraid of crashing!" Troy replied, trying to grin through clenched teeth.

A short while later, another airline stewardess came around with some magazines and snacks. The choice of beverage was pop, water, juice, or alcohol. Lisa took a Cosmopolitan magazine and 2 Pepsi colas and 2 bags of peanuts for both of them. They browsed through the pages of the magazine together, stopping to read an article on working moms and how they juggled family and work. "Remember who's in charge," one interviewed woman commented. "It's all about routine," another woman said.

"How can they write this crap?" Lisa asked.

"Okay, Sweet Cheeks," Troy said, pinching Lisa's cheeks, then kissing them. "Let's make a toast to breaking routine every chance we can get!" They clanged their glasses together and laughed.

"Shall we start in the washroom?" Lisa asked innocently, as the corners of her lips curled in a devilish grin.

Chapter 114

When the young couple landed in Las Vegas, they unloaded their bags onto a cart and went outside to hail a cab.

"Where to?" the Jamaican taxi driver asked politely.

"I thought maybe you could tell us. We're looking for a reasonably priced hotel with a honeymoon suite," Troy replied.

"We're looking for Elvis," Lisa added, poking her head out from between the 2 front seats.

"Honeymoon suite…Elvis…" the Jamaican taxi driver said, making calculations in his head. "Name's Jammi. Have you booked an appointment?"

"Appointment?" Troy asked, taken aback.

"Prebooked weddings with Elvis are cheaper. *On the fly* weddings with Elvis are more expensive."

"We just want to get married by Elvis," Lisa said, folding her arms and pouting like a spoiled brat.

"What am I going to do about all your luggage while you're getting married? Drop it by the curb while you go inside?"

"Hotel, then chapel," Troy said, trying to sound more confident than he felt.

"There's a hotel a few blocks from Sunset Boulevard. You can check in there and I'll help you with your luggage if you want."

"What are we waiting for? Let's go!" Troy said impatiently. The hotel was called the Sunset Villa and was surrounded by hedges and red and white flower beds bordered by white, equal-sized rocks. There was a water fountain with a statue of a little boy pouring a bucket of water. Lisa was reminded of the nursery rhyme, *Jack and Jill*, and wondered where Jill was. She looked around.

The lobby was spacious with marble floors and mirrored walls. Pictures of past presidents were mounted on the wall behind the front desk along with the American flag to spell it out for tourists.

"We'd like a room," Troy said, "with a corporate rate, if possible."

"We'd like the honeymoon suite too," Lisa added.

"You'd like the corporate rate for the honeymoon suite?"

"That's what we just said," Troy and Lisa said in unison, and laughed.

"Are you in the marriage business?" the hotel clerk asked politely.

"Troy works for my father," Lisa said and hugged Troy's arm proudly.

"Is your father in the marriage business then?" the clerk asked, undeterred. Lisa looked at Troy and Troy looked at Lisa. Then Troy produced a $100 bill. He slapped it down on the marble countertop and leaned in close. He thought about grabbing the ballsy clerk by the front of his shirt and pulling him closer, but instead exercised self-control on account of his bride-to-be.

Suddenly the front desk clerk bought himself a whole new attitude. He pocketed the $100 bill gratefully and took down their personal information, then escorted them to the honeymoon suite. "A bellboy will bring up your luggage."

"We haven't paid the cab driver yet," Lisa said anxiously.

"What's your hurry? This is Vegas."

"We can't just keep him waiting like that."

"Of course, take care of it. In the meantime, I'll have room service bring up a fruit tray and a complimentary bottle of champagne."

"Thanks, Oscar," Troy and Lisa said in unison, reading off the hotelier's name tag.

Troy paid the cab driver who was listening to Reggae music that was cranked up loud. "I didn't know the meter was still running. I thought it only ran when the wheels were turning," Troy confessed.

"What part of this planet are you from, bro?" the Jamaican asked, inspecting the money to see if it was real or counterfeit.

"Glendale," Troy replied proudly. "Glendale, Saskatchewan, Canada."

"Here's my business card," Jammi said. "My brother from a different mother is in the marrying business. If you can't find Elvis in the phone book, call this number." Jammi jammed the business card down Troy's front shirt pocket. "Don't lose it," he said to Troy and then his eyes shifted to Lisa and their eyes locked. "Save it for your wedding night," Jammi said, and peeled out of the parking lot. "I'll be your baby's God father!" he shouted into the Las Vegas night where anything seemed possible…

Chapter 115

A week later, Lisa and Troy headed back home. Mr. Conway was waiting for the newlyweds at the airport. "How did it go? Did you find Elvis?" he asked.

"All the Elvis's in the Yellow Pages were booked, but Jammi, our Jamaican cabbie, found us a Jamaican Elvis who married us on the spot," Lisa said brightly.

"Did he sing any Elvis songs?" Mr. Conway asked.

"No, mostly Bob Marley," Troy replied.

"You don't say," Mr. Conway mumbled to himself as he struggled with a suitcase.

Chapter 116

Professor West parked his car and started walking on the hiking trail toward Cedar Falls. He almost walked right past Erno and Nancy without even noticing them. "Wasn't that Professor West?" Erno asked Nancy.

"Do fish swim?"

"What's he doing here?"

"The same as us. Hiking to see Cedar Falls," Nancy replied.

At long last the Falls appeared, barricaded off by a steel link fence to keep tourists from falling to their death The view was breathtaking, so much in fact that the Professor woofed his cookies right then, right there, much to the amazement of a bunch of Japanese tourists with cameras who all turned their cameras on him en masse to catch a white man puking his guts out. "What's your shutter speed set at?" one Japanese tourist asked the other one in Japanese.

"Fast speed…1/125 sec," was the reply, also in Japanese.

"This picture could be Photo of the Year," the first Japanese tourist said. They both bowed.

Professor West dabbed his mouth with a tissue and bowed too. "Heights," he pantomimed. "I'm afraid of heights. Ergo, I go puky-puky," he continued to pantomime.

"Hi, I'm Akira Watanabe and this is Asahi Yamamoto. Sometimes we get together and freelance."

"I didn't know you spoke English."

"You didn't ask," Akira replied, snapping a quickie of the Professor before pushing on.

"You didn't ask!" Professor West shouted after him.

"I'll send you a photo for your autograph!" Asahi promised.

"You do that!" Professor West threatened, giving Asahi Yamamoto the famous *Clink Eastwood squint*. He took a swig of whiskey to freshen his breath and searched for the infamous rainbow in the Falls, but couldn't see it anywhere. *It must be a myth. I had to come here to see that there never was a rainbow, so there never will be a pot of gold at the end of it either.* He took another swig of whiskey, and another.

"Make a wish anyway," the devil whispered in his ear.

"I wish I could fly."

"Then try."

"Sorry, devil, but didn't you use that line on Jesus?"

"Yeah, and he resisted, but look how he ended up."

"Between a murderer and a thief."

"Exactly. What do you do when you're between a rock and a hard place?" the devil whispered in the Professor's other ear.

"I don't know. Why don't I call up Fred Flintstone and ask?" Professor West shouted.

Suddenly he felt a tiny tug on his sleeve. "Who's Fred Flintstone?" a little girl with pigtails asked, tilting her tiny freckled face up toward him.

A small crowd had gathered, whether to see the Falls or a crazy old drunk ranting and raving out loud, no one could say for sure. Nancy rushed toward the Professor. "Professor, you seem a bit off your game today. Are you alright?" Nancy asked compassionately.

"I'll be fine," the Professor said, "just as soon as I get off this mountain. I'm afraid of heights."

By now, Erno had joined up with Nancy. "That's a relief," Erno said. "For a while, we were afraid you were going to jump. You must have a guardian angel who talked you out of it."

"Never let the devil get the upper hand in no man's land," Professor West said to both of them, before heading back down the mountain. He had argued with the devil many times knowing that it was, for better or for worse, a loser's game. He was flawed but didn't want to be rescued because his flaws made him feel alive as nothing else could.

Mary Anne tucked the rough draft of Glendale County under her pillow and fell asleep. The sound of the rustling poplars outside her open window blended in with the voices of the spirit world, telling her that anything was possible *if she only allowed herself to dream…*

THE END